THE KING OF TRASH

DONALD WILLERTON

ROUGH
EDGES
PRESS

THE KING OF TRASH

To
Gerald M. Weinberg,
Author, Teacher, Friend

CHAPTER 1

PARKER EVANS.

I doubt there are many people anywhere on Earth who haven't heard of him. For the last few decades, Parker Evans has been mentioned on a regular basis in every major newspaper around the world: his attending some international conference, his building a new offshore wind farm, his adding a new ocean cleaning platform, quotes from a speech he gave in Zurich, Paris, New York, or Shanghai, or the latest update on his position in the list of the wealthiest people in the world —he's usually on top. And that's not to mention his fame for having received not one but two Nobel Prizes.

Parker is a man of staggering genius, free and clear. I should know because I grew up with the guy. I was there when everything was good times, and I was there when the dead bodies were found.

We were the Mutt and Jeff of Central Elementary in Broad Point, Texas, a little outside Fort Worth. I was big and awkward and destined for the traditional Texas schoolboy track—football—while he was several inches shorter than me and was already the city chess champion. His father was a scientist of some sort, and his mother a psychologist, while my parents taught at the local community college. Our houses were next door to each other. We got together after school, playing guns and war, and wrestling at my house, or playing chess, building things with his erector set, and playing with his hamster at his house. We probably would have stayed friends if his parents hadn't started buying him private tutors. Eventually, he went to a special school in Philadelphia.

I want to state upfront that whenever I'm asked if I ever saw any of the dark side that Parker would later make so clear —the side that resulted in the murdering of thousands and his mental imprisonment by his own psychosis—I readily respond that I did not. He was aggressive about winning at chess and blew up easily the few times he lost. He was hyperactive about reading, which showed his remarkable ability to learn things with almost no effort. He found most social situations, like being surrounded by other grade-school students, irritating and useless. He admitted that I was his closest friend because I was his only friend.

But there was nothing that seemed outside the realm of an ordinary elementary school boy.

Privately, however, I do recall being shocked at Parker's laughing when we fed his hamster a supposed invisibility potion that left it screeching horribly as it slowly choked to death. It was even more abhorrent when he kicked the hamster's body over the fence into my backyard. He told me I could bury it if I wanted to, which I did that night. I didn't tell my parents.

That left me convinced that a certain part of him was definitely tolerant of violence, making a really smart person like him unusually dangerous.

Parker graduated from his special school at fourteen, began MIT in the summer, and had a doctorate in physics before eighteen, and another in chemistry a couple of years later. He was ready for a brilliant career as a professor when an extraordinary accident occurred in his college laboratory.

Meanwhile, I had graduated from high school about the time Parker graduated from his first college. I spent two years playing football at a junior college, then a couple more years at a four-year school where I played long enough to blow out my knee. In the summer, I worked at KFC to help pay expenses. I graduated with a journalism degree and have had a good career writing for magazines and newspapers, so I'm not ashamed of how I turned out, nor am I intimidated by his accomplishments. The world needs geniuses like Parker just like it needs people like me.

Okay, back to the accident.

Parker was at MIT at the time, researching a new kind of chemical core for electric car batteries. Lightning hit the building, a breaker failed, and electricity shot around Parker's chemistry lab, eventually hitting a beaker full of liquid something-or-the-other that was next to an ordinary car battery on the table. Glassware exploded, the battery cracked open, the beaker with Parker's liquid shattered, and the smell was awful. He ran like a rabbit while the whole place smoked up like a trench in World War I. Thankfully, no one was hurt.

When Parker came back into the room, he found that the electric charge had dissolved his liquid into a rubber table pad, while being drenched in chemicals from the battery. With everything mixing together, the result was a thick film that had spread all over his workbench. Trying to clean things up, he found the film could not be removed. The harder he tried, the more it resisted. He realized something extraordinary had happened.

The film had chemically bonded with the workbench. That was interesting, but more interesting was how slick the electrified liquid/rubber/chemical combination had become. We're talking *slick* here—absolutely no surface friction.

Remember when Teflon was first used in the space program? America thought it was only an interesting novelty until they coated a skillet with it, and then everyone went berserk. It made cookware so slick nothing would stick to it. Not burned cheese, not burned eggs, not burned butter, nothing. Everyone in America suddenly wanted Teflon-coated pans and pots.

Parker's new film was way beyond that. It was slickslick-slick. Unbelievably slick. Phenomenally slick.

Realizing what had been made, he abandoned his battery research and devoted himself to understanding his accident. A year later, he had created a liquid version of the film that was thin enough to used in a spray gun. He borrowed money against his trust fund, took over his parents' garage as a laboratory, and started testing.

What eventually became a viable commercial product was a thin film coating that could be sprayed on any metal surface where friction was a problem—like the hull of a steel boat, for example. Parker pulled the family boat out of the water, scraped off the paint, and sprayed on his film. The film bonded with the metal hull, he put it back in the lake, and just like that, it was going twice as fast while using the same motor.

It might take the rest of us a while to figure out what could be done with this discovery, but it didn't take Parker long at all. As soon as he could manage it, he contracted with the Navy to coat the hull of a small cruiser to show what the film could do. The test was a success. The ship practically zoomed through the water, while the Navy projected a clear 18 percent cost saving. The admiral who'd given the experiment the go-ahead was doing backflips.

The next year, Parker rented a drydock near the shipyards in Newport Beach, revamped his process to make it more efficient, and sprayed the hull of a destroyer. Success again! He was soon contracting with a bigger shipyard to work on his first aircraft carrier.

When the carrier set new benchmarks for speed, efficiency, and cost, a landslide of government contracts set Parker up to become very, very rich. Then, as if it wasn't enough, he did something no one expected: he franchised his hull coating business. When the Navy told him his thin film coating was a national security asset that required their total control, Parker had the Supreme Court tell the Navy to go fly a kite. He had invented it and he could choose who used it.

That opened the door to hundreds of shipyards around the world offering ship owners the opportunity to coat their hulls with this miracle product. It made every ship faster, more cost-effective, and the thin film was nearly indestructible. It soon became the standard for shipbuilding. And every time a cash register at any franchised shipyard rang, money slid into Parker Evans's pocket. The money poured in, he put it in the bank, patted himself on the back, received his first Nobel Prize in chemistry, and at the old age of forty, Parker Evans became the richest person in the world.

I'm sure some psychology student has done a research paper about how some rich people became rich—or successful or influential or whatever—because of an accident. That is, it wasn't their genius or smarts or savvy that led to their immense wealth, but some improbable occurance that no one ever expected. Taking advantage of the incident was their true genius, and became the turning point in their success. Parker's accident in the chemistry lab is a good example. If it hadn't happened, he might have lived a long life as an esteemed chemistry professor.

With that in mind, you would think one life-changing accident would be enough for these people. Well, Parker got two. He decided to take a vacation and sail his yacht to Hawaii. Not paying much attention, he casually laid out a route that put him crossing the middle of the Great Pacific Garbage Patch.

Everyone knows about the monstrous areas of trash floating in the North Pacific. The whole circling-current phenomenon extends from the Orient to the US, but there's an oval-shaped section between California and Hawaii that's called the Great Pacific Garbage Patch, where approximately eighty-eight million metric tons of trash are dispersed over an area about twice the size of Texas. The currents swirl whatever's floating on the surface into a circle, like an eddy on a river. It sounds unbelievable, but if you go to YouTube and type in *ocean trash*, the footage is pretty remarkable, especially when the trash escapes the eddy and piles up on a used-to-be beautiful beach.

By far, the major component of all this trash is plastic: water, juice, soda bottles, grocery bags, coffee cup lids, cups, cartons, storage bins, five-gallon buckets, trash cans, plastic knives, forks, spoons, straws, shower curtains, swimming pool floats, Frisbees, toys, kids' swimming pools, car bumpers, boats, rafts, fishing nets, hammocks, computer parts, plumbing pipes, and on and on and on.

Plastic is found in every culture in the world. After its useful life, it typically ends up in garbage dumps, landfills, or as litter throughout the countryside. Not that recycling doesn't make a difference, but worldwide, the problem is growing far faster than changing social behaviors can address. For example, more plastic was made in the first decade of this century than in all of history before then.

Each year, 8 million metric tons of plastic get added to the 150 million tons already in the world's oceans. Most of it starts out on land but is then carried to the sea by way of rain or floods washing trash into rivers. Ten major rivers account for 90 percent of the world's aquatic pollution—by huge rainy seasons, and by tsunamis, typhoons, and hurricanes that scour whole cities of unimaginable quantities of stuff, sucking it all out to sea. It's estimated that up to 20 percent of the current North Pacific trash can be traced back to the Fukushima tsunami of 2011.

Okay, let's get back to Parker. He eventually found himself sailing in floating trash for days. Not being content to just look, Parker used a long-handled landing net to pull up enough floating debris to fill a garbage bag. Noticing an offensive slime covering everything, he borrowed a pair of pantyhose from his then-current girlfriend—she wouldn't last long, a woman who brings pantyhose on a sailboat wasn't his kind of woman—and then cut the net from the handle, and bent the metal loop until he could stretch the pantyhose across it. He dipped it in the Pacific. It came out filled with globs of noxious sludge. He immediately realized that he was looking at the real pollution of the ocean.

I described the *you-can-see-it* forms of plastic floating on the ocean. As horrible as that is, those forms are not the deadly side of plastic in the ocean. The deadly side is that plastic degrades.

One empty plastic water bottle floating in the water is something that can be seen and collected. But one empty plastic water bottle floating in the water for a long time tends to come apart: the constant beating of the waves and the exposure to solar radiation makes it crack, shrink, splinter, shatter, rip, and shred. One empty bottle disintegrates into a hundred pieces of plastic. Each of the pieces continues to degrade, breaking apart and getting smaller and smaller, until the one empty plastic bottle becomes a million tiny pieces of plastic.

Most fish typically can't swallow a whole plastic bottle. But a good portion of the million tiny pieces of degraded plastic are the size of plankton, the tiny organisms that are the base of the food chain for a wide variety of marine animals.

Fish that ingest plankton as their food source can't distinguish it from plastic, and swallow both.

Researchers have found seven hundred fifty thousand microplastic pieces per square kilometer in the Great Pacific Garbage Patch, and the marine animals in that part of the ocean have intestines full of them. In parts of the Patch, the tiny plastic pieces are so thick in the water that they act as a colloidal layer from inches to hundreds of feet thick. Think of all the suspended flecks when you shake up a bottle of Italian salad dressing. Imagine a tuna swimming for days in that mess, and then imagine that tuna on your plate.

Parker, who had heard of the Garbage Patch, was not surprised by the amount of floating trash he saw, but he hadn't realized the prevalence of the deadly microscopic plastic pollution until the pantyhose came out of the water. He was horrified and disgusted and intrigued. By the time he docked in Hawaii, he had found a new calling and set about engineering a solution to one of the world's largest and most crippling problems.

Parker knew the big pieces of trash were manageable. That is, you could line up a thousand ships dragging regular fishing nets across the top of the water and essentially scour the big pieces from the ocean's surface. But that wouldn't touch the plastic Italian salad dressing. He then theorized dragging a zillion pairs of pantyhose, but they would fill up in seconds and had significant logistical problems, including having to dispose of all those gunky pairs of pantyhose.

How about a single pair of pantyhose that was very, very, very large?

Well, he reasoned, even if you could create some kind of net made of the same nylon fabric as pantyhose, but a thousand feet across, it would certainly catch a lot of those teeny-tiny pieces of plastic but would also snare thousands of fish, turtles, and whales. Besides that, it would be the ocean equivalent of tugging a parachute through the water. A vessel the size of an aircraft carrier would be needed to make any headway, but even a fleet of aircraft carriers pulling nets wouldn't solve the problem of disposing of the stuff once the nets fill up.

What was needed was a net that let the fish, turtles, and other marine life pass through, but still trapped the tiny pieces of plastic. That is, it had to have openings that were both big and tiny at the same time. To the rest of us, this is impossible —a single opening can't be both big enough for fish to escape and tiny enough that microplastic pieces wouldn't.

But Parker Evans didn't win a Nobel Prize by being second in his class. He realized that he already had a miracle film in his hull coating, and all he needed was to find the right kind of flexible fabric to spray the film onto. That would make the fabric slick, much easier to pull through the water, and as tough as it needed to be for the ocean environment. That left the problem of needing holes in the fabric that were both big and tiny at the same time. Again, to you and me, impossible.

Allow me to jump over the year of research and development that came next.

Parker Evans developed a filtration fabric that was a marvel of chemistry and electricity. Never finding a flexible fabric that would work, he created his own fabric by making a thick, stand-alone sheet of his miracle hull coating and punching it full of large uniformly spaced holes.

He then sandwiched electrical wires between two of the sheets with wires circling each hole, all connected to common electrical cables, and gluing the two sheets together. When he energized the sandwiched sheets by making a strong electric current flow through the wires around each hole, a magnetic field was created across the hole's opening. Once that happened, anything that had a magnetic field of its own would be repelled by the hole's magnetic field and wouldn't pass through. Living things, which aren't good conductors and don't have inherent magnetic fields, would pass through the hole with no problems.

The problem was that plastic isn't a conductor; it won't react to an electric charge or a magnetic field. From my point of view, Parker had swapped one impossible problem for another, but stick with me here.

He made a mental jump no one else anticipated: It didn't matter if the individual microplastic pieces were conductors or not. If the colloid—the sludge made up of the little plastic pieces—*acted* like a conductor, then it would work. In fact, the thicker the plastic Italian salad dressing, the better it acts like a conductor, and thus would have an induced magnetic field of its own, due to its movement through the earth's magnetic field. That made the colloid resistant to going through the electrified holes of the fabric. Big stuff went through, tiny stuff did not.

Yeah, I didn't understand that part either. No Nobel Prize for me. Let's move on.

A few experiments, some sea trials and Parker finally found the right combination of hole size, electrical charge, and fabric thickness. The net he created was amazingly successful. It prevented the out-flow of tiny plastic pieces while allowing small marine animals and plankton to escape. Now, he had to make it work on a scale appropriate for an ocean.

That's just engineering, Parker was heard to say.

CHAPTER 2

MY PART in this story begins with my coming to work one morning and passing two homeless men who had set up camp under the building's entrance portico. I stopped at the editor's desk as soon as I got through the door.

"What do you want me to do about it?" he asked.

"We have security people, right? You're the editor. Call them, and have them tell those people to go someplace else."

"I don't think they'll find a better place. They've got protection from the wind and the rain. I'm not surprised they chose to be where they are."

I wasn't in his office to debate the subject. "That's irrelevant. They shouldn't be using our entrance to dump their junk and spend the night. It looks bad, and who knows if they're not psycho or something. It looks unfriendly to visitors, and probably to the people who work here. If we don't get rid of them, they'll come back, and then someone in the building's going to start bringing them donuts every morning, and someone else will ask them to have a cup of coffee in the break room. It's a slippery slope, and we shouldn't get started."

All I got in response was a thoughtful look. "You know,"

the boss said, "I wonder about those people: who they are, why they live in the streets, what got them there."

Then he paused—a pause I immediately knew was dangerous for me. I was thinking I should have sent him an email or a text or left him a note. Or even better, contacted security myself. Or maybe just gone into my office, closed the door, and went on with my ordinary life.

Instead, I said, "Those are great questions, Mike, but aren't you a little scared by them? I mean, think about our safety here. If they're high on drugs and we do something like hit them with a door accidentally when we open it, who knows what kind of confrontation they could launch into, or maybe even pull a gun."

He had stood and was looking out the window at the two men and their meager collection of clothes, bags, and blankets.

"They don't look like terrorists," Mike finally said, "although you have a point. I don't think the word compassion is anywhere in the employee handbook."

It was a bad sign when he said that word.

"You know, maybe there's a story here," he went on. "I'll bet our readers don't know anything about these street people or homeless or whatever they are. Maybe what we need is a good, respected reporter to talk to these people, find out who they are, what their story is, and how they ended up sleeping on our front porch. And then let the rest of us know what he found out."

That's when he turned to me with a smile.

Damn.

———

THE TWO RAGGED men on the porch were gone by the time I finished typing up another story I had a deadline for. I hadn't wanted to talk to them anyway. If they didn't like what I wrote, I'd have to start coming in the back door to avoid them. I needed to find another approach.

There were plenty of choices. Most major intersections had people holding signs asking for a handout, panhandlers were all over the sidewalks downtown, and it would be easy to find a homeless camp under some overpass. I had been to a shelter for a story once, and there were always the missions, food centers, and churches that could point me to someone to interview.

Jimmy A was my first choice because he looked safe and was often around my neighborhood. He was a wiry kind of guy, short, and with a neat beard glaring white against his black skin. I guessed he was around seventy or so. He always wore his long-sleeve shirt tucked in, belt cinched up, shoes tied, and ball cap hiding his thinning head of hair. His eyes were clear and bright, and he usually had a smile. Definitely a street person, but he looked better than most.

Most mornings, he'd be holding a sign on a corner down from my house, hoping someone would roll down their window to give him a dollar or some loose change. Other times, I'd glimpse him hoofing it from one place to another, or sitting in a park smoking a cheap cigarillo. He carried an old daypack with a worn coat tied up with a rope over his shoulder for cold mornings. I saw no reason to be afraid of him.

"How long have you been on the streets?" I asked.

Jimmy sat back against the building, took a long suck on his cigar, closed one eye, and let out a tight stream of smoke. "Oh, well, close to twenty years, on and off, I guess."

I held my breath against the smoke. "What put you on the streets to start with?"

He coughed a laugh. "Oh, I got a powerful tearjerker of a

story, but there's no need to go into it. I wore it out a long time ago. I'm here now 'cause I've got everything I need. Most times, anyway."

"You're on the street because you want to be?"

"Well, my choices are slim to none, let's say, not that I'm complaining. Too old for anyone to hire, too dumb for computers, too old to learn anything, too much arthritis in my knees to stand up much, too itchy to stay in one place for long, can't stand to take orders from some yahoo who wants to reform me or improve me or something like that. I guess I could sweep buildings or parking lots, but I get by as well working the corners here. Got a sweet place to sleep every night, and people mostly leave me alone. I'm riding a smooth rail right now."

"You're happy?"

He coughed again, pulled a leg up, and wrapped his arms around it. "I got good days and bad, like most people. Ain't no way to lie about liking rain or wind or cold weather. 'Course, I stay home covered up if it's real bad outside. The bad part's not bein' able to go anywhere. I can't sleep too much before I gotta get up and move around to get the hurts out. You know we get bored? I bet people never think of us street folk getting bored. It don't bother me if I got a good book to read or maybe a pile of magazines, but I'd rather be out doin' something."

Mostly, he was right. Ordinary people probably don't think of Streeters—the label my mind started giving them—as being bored.

Lazy, maybe. Crazy, probably. Looking for handouts because they don't want to work or can't, sure. Dangerous. Sick. Desperate. I don't think people refuse to have sympathy for the poor and homeless, but we want a cause for it: forced poverty, tight job market, lack of education, PTSD, jail time, drugs, age, exhaustion, mental illness, language barriers. Finding a reason—or maybe an excuse—gives us permission to notice them and maybe have a little compassion. It lets us think it's not something that was under their control.

"Any family?"

Another tight stream of grayish-white cloud. "A couple of kids, but they're back in Indiana, or were, last I heard. When my wife died of cancer years ago, the kids didn't like the empty house, I guess, so they asked to move in with my brother, and I let them. I worked at a tool factory, just doing maintenance and stuff, but the job moved to Mexico, and I had only the mortgage left, and an empty neighborhood, so I sold the house, gave the kids the money, and went west. Go west, young man, ain't that what they say? Well, I went west, then went back east. The West sucks. I sold the car to pay for a room and food while I looked for work, but it disappeared like it had wings. Pretty soon, I was outta money, and the streets were the only thing left. I hung around different towns, but the weather kind of drives everything. Here, the seasons are pretty nice, the buses get me around, and when I found a sweet place to camp, I decided to stay. I consider myself retired, though I doubt the city agrees with me. I think about my kids now and then—my brother too, I really do—but I don't fit in anymore. I'm sure my kids who—damn, must be in their 30s or 40s by now—are doing just fine without me."

"Tell me about living on the street," I said.

"Oh, well, there's the freedom to move around. It's probably overrated, but it is what it is. I don't owe anybody anything, don't have to follow anyone's orders, don't need a schedule 'cause there's no place I have to be. And there's nice people hereabouts, mostly. I visit, talk to people, keep my ear to the ground for new places to eat and such. There's a little barbershop on Fourth Street that gives free haircuts to folks like me, so I keep my hair trimmed and try to wear clean clothes and smile, so people aren't afraid too much."

"New places to eat?"

"That's the dumpsters when a new restaurant opens up. They make big portions to impress people, and lots of stuff is left over. Real good eating for a couple of months or so, then it's over and I go back to the regular dumpsters. It's amazing what people throw away. One year, I actually gained weight."

"Do you have a regular route? Corners you always work? A favorite sign you hold?"

That got him laughing, which made it easier to talk. I like someone who finds humor in hard places.

"You're talking business management skills now. Yep, I got me a routine for regular days, then I do a little different on weekends. I do specials on holidays, like wearin' a hat or ringin' a bell for Christmas. I always limp on Veterans Day," he chuckled. "No Army for me, though. Came in between wars and thought my future was too bright to waste on the military."

The cigarillo was getting short. He took a couple of small puffs and seemed to be looking far away. Jimmy needed to get back to work. I'd made a mental note to buy him a pack of those cigarillos some morning.

Respected reporter, the boss had called me. At fifty-seven, I've been in the newspaper business thirty-two years, doing mostly everything—crime, politics, sports, obits, schools, government—long enough to graduate into writing weekly columns. Now, I do investigative work, which means anything that takes more than a couple of days to figure out and write up. Usually, it's stuff like political shenanigans at City Hall, or construction projects that never get finished, or patients waiting forever at the V.A. or even a new business coming to town—how it's good for some people and bad for others.

When those things are slow, the boss pretty much gives me free rein for whatever catches my interest, as long as it has to do with life in the city and I get it in on time.

But there are days when he finds something for me out of his own head, like the homeless story. I didn't mind the assignment, but it was going to take leg work, and I'd been hoping to coast for the summer, maybe put some of my over-time towards a long vacation or something. Maybe a cruise for me and my wife, Beth, something we could kick back and enjoy and let other people take care of us for a change. Fifty-seven isn't old—though I admit to getting older—but I'm trying to relax more, stay fit, and pay a bit more attention to enjoying life.

I knew another reason why Mike wanted to do the story. It was timely. The city had just passed a law against giving money to panhandlers, or to people with an empty coffee cup or upside-down hat on the sidewalk. The law was stopped in court at the moment, but the issue was still hot, especially with the tourist season being close and the city being concerned about its image. No one thought the law was going to deal with the problem. It was just something to make it less visible, figuring that if tourists in the more popular parts of town didn't give money to the panhandlers, they'd go beg someplace else in town, and the tourists would spend more.

Mike and I figured I could talk to a fair number of the homeless, in addition to city officials and community organi-zations who were trying to help them, and put together a series that could run a half-page, plus photos, in the Sunday paper for three weeks. It was a pretty complicated topic, but a little understanding never hurt anybody. We hoped I would be able to make the homeless a little more human to our readers, clarify some of the issues, and perhaps identify some possible solutions.

Jimmy A was open about his daily circuit, his friends and associates, and his favorite dumpsters, plus his opinions about the local shelters for the homeless and social programs that had reached out to him, but he never told me where his sweet place was, though he enjoyed bragging about it. His home, he said, is a cheap, semi-collapsed, Sears-type metal storage shed tucked into an empty lot behind an industrial building. It's camouflaged by weeds, old cars, and piles of junk, and he doesn't think anyone knows he lives there.

It was clear Jimmy was an ingenious guy. He'd put down several layers of cardboard for a floor and brought in a big refrigerator box to give himself a less drafty bedroom. An old sleeping bag, a slab of discarded foam rubber, a tiny flashlight, a discarded beer cooler to keep the mice out of his food, and he was set. He also had a five-gallon bucket and toilet seat in the corner for a commode if he couldn't get to the gas station two blocks away. He gets broken sacks of unused kitty litter out of the dumpster behind PetSmart so the smell isn't too bad, and he empties it regularly.

Shelter, a dry floor, a comfy bed, a private place to poop. A sweet place, like he said.

"What do you do with the money people give you?" I asked him.

"Oh, I pretty much spend everything I get," he said, taking another long draw. "Gotta have my smokes, you know what I mean?

"And beer. Don't drink much anymore 'cause it hurts if I drink too fast, but I cheat sometimes because nothing beats a cold beer on a hot day. And there's my morning coffee, of course. If someone doesn't hand me a cup, then I get one at the Quick Stop. And maybe a donut. I don't mind buying some of my friends a donut or coffee or something. I always try to remember there's always somebody worse off than me."

Sometimes he'd go to a shelter downtown to take a shower, have a meal, and maybe get some medicines. When there was a stretch of freezing nights, he'd accept a free bed, but he wouldn't stay after the weather warmed. Too crowded, too confining, too public. And too much danger.

"That's why people drag those damned shopping carts all over. There's always someone gonna steal anything you got— and not for the stuff, 'cause it's all worthless. They do it to put fear into you, 'cause they want you to be afraid of them."

Jimmy relaxed against the side of the building, scratching his beard, brushing the ashes off his shirt, and taking meditative puffs on his cigarillo. When he ground the ash into the ground and stuffed the butt into his pocket, my time was up.

When I first started on this series about the homeless, I was curious, like most of us. They seem interchangeable, sitting or standing on corners, holding up signs, buttressed against storefronts by awkward bundles of blankets, looking desperate. Once in a while, we give them money, usually followed by a reply of *God Bless*. We vary between feeling irritated at seeing them and feeling guilty for giving only a dollar when we just spent six bucks on a cup of coffee. Sometimes we have questions: How did they end up there? Do they really need the money? Are they just too lazy to work? Where do they sleep? How can she afford cigarettes? Why is there always a dog? Is he really a vet? Aren't there social programs for these people? Why don't they use them? If I give them money, will they buy food, or drugs and smokes?

We're curious, but we're also compassionate. Most of us have had hard times, or our families have, living paycheck to paycheck, one more bad thing and we're over the edge, job in danger, crushed by debt, trapped by medical bills, no light at the end of the tunnel.

We've been there, or damned close. We have empathy, so we reach into our pockets for that dollar.

But we're also wary—not wanting to be made fools of, as well as sometimes being scared too. We hate being deceived, we hate being suckers, and we really hate being victims. Couldn't the government be taking care of these people? Doesn't it have shelters? Isn't that part of what I'm paying taxes for? Aren't there programs, food banks, soup kitchens? What about the Salvation Army, the V.A., the churches?

We assume someone out there is helping them. Someone must be. But we don't ever ask because we don't really want to know.

IN LOS ANGELES, the number of homeless people rose twenty-three percent in 2017. An estimated sixty thousand people within the city limits alone have no adequate housing on a nightly basis. In adjacent Orange County, a tent community stretched for miles next to what had been a popular walking, jogging, and biking path. After an uproar from nearby residents, the county unceremoniously forced the occupants off the land while maintenance crews tore down more than seven hundred ramshackle dwellings—mostly tents and tarps—leaving behind two hundred fifty tons of trash, eleven hundred pounds of human waste, and five thousand hypodermic needles.

San Francisco, which has a far smaller number of homeless, reportedly budgeted $240 million in 2017 to build and run housing and treatment centers for them—an average of $32,000 for each of the city's estimated 7,499 homeless residents. In spite of this, national organizations concerned about their members' safety have moved conferences to other cities.

Every year, municipal authorities receive thousands of complaints about human waste in public places.

The Department of Housing and Urban Development estimates that in the United States, more than six hundred thousand people are homeless every day. Most of them try to sleep in either a homeless shelter or some sort of short-term transitional housing. Slightly more than a third spend the night in cars, or under bridges, or in some other way are unsheltered.

One-quarter of the homeless in the US are children.

CHAPTER 3

IT TOOK me a couple of weeks to finish the three articles about the homeless. In general, they were well-received, shaking up not only the general public but also several social organizations around the city, lighting an unwanted fire under the seats of people who really wanted to ignore the whole situation.

My only regret was that I could not, truthfully, zero in on any solutions. Homelessness is a hugely difficult problem, with physical, financial, mental, logistical, and medical concerns that have to be balanced for every individual. I became familiar with most of the relevant federal, state, and local responses to the problems of the homeless, but none seemed to make much difference to the sort of people I had interviewed. Most were shooting arrows at the wrong target.

I was further disappointed in not finding a personal solution for myself. The grassroots approach to solving problems that I typically adopt, valuing the contribution of individuals who decide to work out things on their own, did me no good. I couldn't find anything I could personally do to help that didn't demand more time, effort, money, or all three than I was willing to give. While I readily admit I'm not going to invite a homeless person to move into my house, I had expected to find something more useful to do than just handing out my loose change.

Nonetheless, I was happy with the articles and was moving on with the rest of my workload when my editor decided that the paper needed a follow-up article.

"What's the other side of this," he asked me one day. "Isn't there anything positive going on, anything useful someone's doing?"

I told him I'd find out.

A few days later, I reported back: "Sorry, boss, not much. There's a kid in San Diego getting a lot of press about putting people to work cleaning up the city, and some enclave outside Austin is giving mini-houses to the homeless and putting them to work in a subsistence garden. A little local success, maybe here and there, but that's about it. Homelessness, poverty—it's tough. Most big cities can't do much that makes any difference."

"How about anyplace else? Some other country? Isn't anyone anywhere doing something on a bigger scale? What about the UN?"

That made me think of Parker. "Well, if you want to talk globally, you know Parker Evans? He's got an idea about changing the upstream conditions and social structure to more or less prevent poverty and homelessness in the first place. He's got a whole community down in Mexico called Nuevo Mundo that's running off his ocean cleaning operation. He gets enough plastic from the Pacific to make electricity that powers the surrounding countryside for hundreds of miles. From what I hear, they don't have poverty or homelessness or transient problems or even drugs. Everyone swears it's a miracle.

"It's not that far. I could go down and check it out. It sounds like it works, and on a pretty big scale."

"Yeah, okay." Mike nodded his head. He told me to take a week and come back with something that would make a Sunday series like the first homeless articles. I figured I could do it easy, and work up a pretty good tan while I was at it.

Which brings us back to Parker.

After engineering his ocean-worthy miracle, the thick-film-with-wires-and-holes method of filtering the plastic out of seawater, Parker Evans invented, developed, and put in place a number of floating trash-gathering platforms in the different Garbage Patches around the world. The platforms spent their time scooping up big hunks of floating trash, the visible trash, and filtering the seawater through his fabric for as much plastic sludge, the invisible trash, as possible. They then shoved the visible and invisible trash into huge, specially-made cylindrical tubes, sealed the end, and pushed them into the ocean with beacons on top. A collection ship, usually a recycled container ship, latched onto the floating tubes and pulled them aboard. Since they looked suspiciously like forty-foot-long sausages, that's what they're called as the ships brought them to land-based facilities for processing.

The collection ships for the eastern Pacific hauled their sausages to Mexico, to what Parker had called Nuevo Mundo, on the Baja peninsula. The sausages were emptied on huge concrete drying floors to sift burnable material from unburnable material. The burnable, mostly plastic, was scooped up after drying in the hot Mexican sun for a week and taken by conveyor belt to industrial-sized furnaces ten miles away. The petroleum-based plastic was burned as fuel in the furnaces, producing steam that drives turbines to produce electricity in a generation plant next door. The electricity is then sold remarkably cheaply to the host country—in this case, Mexico, but there were similar facilities along the coasts of Africa, India, and Australia. As for what Mexico did with the power, its people definitely benefited, but the government also made money selling the electricity at a much higher price to American cities along the border.

The whole operation occupies a large slice of the Baja, for no other reason than the drying trash smells awful. Really awful. Like rotting fish awful. That's why the drying floors are located in the remotest area possible. If you consider there's usually two or three dozen sausages' worth of drying trash at any one time, it is one serious stench.

My job would be to fly to the facility in Mexico, get the details, and tie the whole business in with my homeless articles by interviewing the locals of the community and contrasting the differences in our policies, processes, and outcomes.

It was an interesting and worthwhile idea for the paper, but I also thought that if I could get on Parker's radar, I might get a book deal out of it. Several books had already been written about his life, but I was betting I could get some unique stories out of the time we were kids. I was tired of always being on deadline anyway, and that vacation I mentioned was sounding better and better. I needed a transition plan for the future, and writing a book would fit right in.

———

AFTER A FLIGHT to San Diego and a long day's drive south, I boarded a helicopter with Raymond Armijo, the general manager of the Nuevo Mundo complex.

"This place is huge!" I yelled into the microphone on my headset.

We had flown over the plant and furnaces and were looking down now at the drying floors next to the trash processing facility. They looked like miles and miles of airport runways.

"When they were built," Armijo responded, "the drying

floors used more concrete than O'Hare in Chicago, and had enough track—for the automated cranes—to build a railroad across California."

He pointed down at what looked like junior-sized versions of the harbor cranes that load and unload container ships.

"There are fifty-four cranes moving the sausages around," he said. "Each one is self-powered, controlled by software. A central control tower coordinates the operation and oversees the distribution network, but everything is self-guided. See in the distance, over there? That's the pickup point where the sausages come off the collection ships and go onto a conveyor belt. Each crane is programmed to pick a sausage up off the belt and take it along the rails to the right dumping point. The sausage is lowered, the end opened up, then the crane lifts it and backs away so the insides slide out onto the concrete."

"What's the purpose of the yellow on some of the sausages?" I asked.

"When the trash is handled at the cleaning platform on the ocean," Armijo said, "it's separated into sausages that will hold the compacted sludge and small trash, while others, marked with yellow, have trash that can't be compacted, like pieces of wood or barrels or old fishing nets. Dividing the big stuff out at the source makes it easier for us to sort whatever comes."

He pointed back at the runways.

"The plastic and other burnable material is dried and taken to the furnaces. The metals and unburnable materials are taken offsite for recycling, and whatever can't be recycled goes into a lined landfill. We monitor the groundwater all around the landfill to make sure we're not polluting the soil. On the other side of the complex is a factory where we mix a binder with the ash byproducts from the furnaces to make bricks."

The level of environmental care was impressive. The state-of-the-art furnaces were highly efficient, releasing almost no particulates into the atmosphere, while the electrical plant was ultra-modern and clean, with none of the risks of nuclear plants. Like the other places he had put his facilities, Parker's host country was responsible for building the power distribution network, but he helped them fund it. If you're thinking he couldn't possibly make a profit at this, you're right. Parker made no bones about the fact that he bankrolls everything with the goal of consuming all the trash he brings in, making as much electricity as possible, and generating enough income to support all the people working there. Any money left over is his, which, if nothing else, makes him a very popular guy.

We flew over the personnel compound.

Employees? Several hundred, all living in a small city designed and built by Parker's corporation. There were offices, training facilities, dorms, apartments, condos, a few houses, a movie theater, a grocery, some shops, an immense cafeteria, ball fields, a swimming pool, an imitation Walmart, a hospital, and a range of schools for family members young and old.

And—the point of what I'd set out to report—his focus on the upstream issues of economy, education, and living conditions had brought pretty dramatic downstream results: no unemployment, no panhandlers, no vagrants, no begging in the streets, no homelessness—in short, no poverty. Everyone works either at Parker's facilities, for the city itself, at service businesses in town, or doing domestic work. Every household is required to use cleaners, cooks, or childcare workers so there are always low-level jobs available. Training programs are offered for those who want to go elsewhere in Mexico to work.

The flight ended, I thanked Armijo, was escorted to a Holiday Inn-ish hotel, and the next day began interviewing employees for my story. I had access to any part of the plant and compound.

Summing up my dull findings, the interviews found a happy, vibrant, and energetic community. The workers were competent, well-trained, and well-rewarded. Their home lives seemed satisfying as well. Most of Nuevo Mundo's children went on to college, and Mexico even offered scholarships to high schools throughout the country for on-site job training at the complex.

I had never written about a project this size with no obvious downsides. Even Greenpeace loved the place. The workers appeared to have full lives, and strict policies banned drugs, guns, and public intoxication. When violations happened, there seemed to be a swift, sure, and transparent local process of justice. Parker Evans seems to be the perfect global partner: gracious and tough, exacting and responsible.

Unfortunately, I learned, he never visits his facility in Mexico; he can't stand the smell.

There went my book.

CHAPTER 4

SALLY B WAS someone else I interviewed for my Streeter articles. She was clearly mentally ill—not dangerous or unbalanced enough to be institutionalized but clearly deserving of her local nickname, Crazy Sally. Within her local community, she was treated as mildly disabled. People were helpful and tolerant, though I doubt she had any true friends. Outside the community, she generated complaints and fear.

As reluctant as Jimmy was to give his down-and-out story, Sally was the opposite, not shy at all, a cheerful conversationalist in a language that was mostly unprintable. Kept in childhood poverty by an abusive father and a drunken mother, she was on her own by twelve and pregnant by fourteen.

After her daughter was stillborn a year later, someone decided she should be sterilized, but she doesn't remember much about the operation. She had few friends in school and dropped out as soon as she could, was enslaved for a period by drugs and alcohol, played at being a prostitute for a while, then drifted into the streets with nowhere to go and nothing to do. She's bipolar but gets drugs from a local clinic to help keep it under control.

When I interviewed her, she was a mid-30s wanderer in

filthy clothes, pushing a shopping cart in which she collects aluminum cans to sell to the Kiwanis on Saturday morning. I don't think she knows how to read.

She worries about money more than Jimmy. Because she's younger, she's constantly looking for little jobs: sacking groceries, sweeping parking lots, rounding up shopping carts, helping direct parking at the local coliseum, or doing odd jobs for a nearby church. I could never find out how she spends her money, but she never seemed to have any.

She once lived with a community of women in a shelter but was nervous and suspicious around the others. When someone stole her soap and the shelter wouldn't do anything about it, the confrontations got aggressive, and she was asked to move on. It is easy to be afraid of her.

Sally would rather be on the streets than in a shelter. She wanders a regular route, eats from regular trash bins and food lines, and sleeps in the woods or dry culverts, keeping her shopping cart roped to her foot. A tent would be better, but someone—maybe the city, she thinks—steals them when she's not there. She's had partners, both male and female, but nothing lasted long. Talking to her isn't unpleasant, unless she gets a full head of steam and slides into fits of shouting.

She wears a bright yellow bandanna around her hair, which she says gives her a competitive advantage because she's easier to recognize. I had to agree. If I was hiring someone to move traffic cones around a parking lot for an event, I'd be able to pick the bandanna out from the others standing in line wanting the job. I assume she gets preferential treatment.

Crazy Sally was on the outer rim of my interviewees with regard to where, how, and why they lived on the streets. As I talked with people, I mentally sorted them: those who were doing just fine, others who needed help from a shelter or the V.A. or food stamps to get by, some who were honestly working to improve their lifestyle—and probably wouldn't be homeless long—and those who were circling the drain. Sally was in the last category, which is to say that I saw no hope she'd ever rejoin regular society or hold a substantial job for very long. Putting her under any kind of restraint, like in an institution, would only be a hateful punishment for things over which she has no control. That means she's destined to be a long-term dependent of the state, and if her housing were to be provided, for example, it would have to be provided until she died.

Jimmy knew her as a friend, and shared what he had with her, but agreed that she was best left alone. Someday, he said, she'll mindlessly walk in front of a car, and that will be that.

I looked for her to interview a second time, but she was not to be found. Everyone said she had simply disappeared. Jimmy thought she'd impulsively joined up with a group of itinerants and hit the road, or maybe had died and they'd dumped her body in a shallow grave in the desert.

I was beginning the last of my articles and thought her death, if it could be confirmed, would make a nice sidebar. I tried the usual places she hung out, checked the coroner's office, and went to fill out a missing person's report at the police. Having never asked her last name, I wasn't too successful. My description of her could fit half the female Streeters in the city.

But of course, even if I knew her name, it wouldn't have done any good. The police can't stop someone for leaving home, not returning to a known area, or doing anything else that wasn't illegal.

They needed a body to consider anything a homicide.

The police report was filed away.

———

IN 1980, roughly a hundred fifty thousand people in the US were reported missing. The number is now nine hundred thousand per year, which is more than twenty-four hundred adults and children every day.

An estimated eight million children worldwide go missing each year: forty thousand in Brazil, thirty-nine thousand in France, a hundred thousand in Germany, and forty-five thousand in Mexico. An estimated two hundred thirty thousand children go missing in the UK every year—one every three minutes. Though many of these children around the world leave home voluntarily and are found within a couple of days, millions more are forced against their will into a life on the streets.

CHAPTER 5

A COUPLE of weeks after the articles about the Mexico operation were published, I got an email. I'd been invited to interview Parker Evans, in the middle of the Pacific, on his personal cruise ship connected to one of his ocean trash-gathering platforms. I didn't jump up and down because I might have hurt myself, but I was pretty excited. I could see myself getting the summer cruise ship experience I'd been thinking about—lounging around a swimming pool in a towel-draped chair, working on my tan, and getting all the naps I richly deserve. And food—oh yes, there would be lots of food.

Parker apparently liked my reporting on his trash-fed electrical plant in Mexico. Not only did I get the interview, but he also asked that I write matching articles about the ocean cleaning side of the process. Together, they'd provide a complete picture of his business, and I suspected his PR department would combine the articles into a glossy marketing brochure. I was fine with that; they'd have to put my name on it somewhere, and it would be a sizable star on my résumé.

His comments, request, and invitation, however, came

from his secretary, so I didn't know if he even realized who I was—or who I had been in his past.

PARKER'S first ocean cleaning platform was called the *Sea Sweep 1.0,* and became operational more than a decade ago. He always called it his favorite platform and kept his personal offices on the cruise ship that housed the platform's workers and served as its control hub. Needing to stay close to his private jet on Oahu, he kept the platform circling in the current a few hundred miles northeast of Hawaii, in the middle of the major concentration of the Great Pacific Garbage Patch. This put him only a few hours away from the rest of the world in case he was ever called on to participate.

The first part of my trip was flying commercially to Hawaii, and now I was enjoying the thrill of zooming above the waves in Parker's private helicopter, watching the swells below as they rippled and merged with each other. An hour or so later, we crossed into an ocean that looked sick. The surface was speckled by the dingy rubble of pieces of floating trash, riding up and down with the waves, impervious to any pretense of ocean might or majesty. Typically luminescent with greens and blues and whites, the water resembled a thick layer of multicolored bathtub scum. As many pictures as I'd seen of trash floating in every direction, its reality was still unnerving.

As we drew closer to the platform, an ocean squall shrouded the helicopter. We flew through machine gun blasts of rain until the ship was below us. Circling it, I realized that as large as any cruise ship might be, the landing pad on the top was still a mighty small target.

I held my breath as the pilot hovered over the giant *H*, its white lines fading in and out as the wind pushed us up and down, the surface twisting and pitching as the ship bucked against the waves and the rain slapping the windows.

The pilot stayed focused on the landing pad below, his hands and eyes sensing the wind, the waves, and the movements of the ship. He brought the chopper closer, timing its movements to the ship's rise and fall as if dancing with the pad's surface. Then—just at the crest of a movement—he set the helicopter down as if it was a calm summer day.

"Hell of a day for a visit," he yelled over the noise as crewmen outside quickly secured the chopper with straps. I took a long breath, unbuckled, and carefully stepped down onto the deck, holding onto my hat and bag as the wind and rain whipped around me. Once the squall passed, the helicopter would return to Oahu. It would be back in four days to pick me up.

Peter Van Thiem, the operations officer, met me with an umbrella.

He was small but looked athletic and strong, and walked with an easy confidence. He seemed full of authority as crew members deferred when they passed him. I guessed he was Thai or Vietnamese, possibly Filipino, and was pretty sure he was Parker's second-in-command. He exuded a military-like kick-your-ass demeanor.

We walked down a stairway to a reception area for passengers waiting for their flights. I was given a short safety briefing, shown diagrams of the ship, was issued an ID card and lanyard to hang around my neck, and fitted with a thick fabric bracelet that wrapped around my wrist. It had a watch face in the center and metallic discs on each side.

"Never take this off," Van Thiem said as he gave me the wristband. "It's a speakerphone. We use it for announcements or directions. It broadcasts an emergency signal if it's submerged in seawater for more than thirty seconds, so if you fall overboard, we can find you."

"And," he smiled, "it will also tell you what time it is. Let's go see Mr. Evans."

The *Sea Sweep* was a true cruise ship, a monster of a vessel just like the ones advertising Caribbean getaways. Walking down football-field-length hallways, Van Thiem pointed out the swimming pool and hot tubs on the upper deck, the immense kitchen, two formal dining rooms, a small casino with an array of slot machines, a bar, eating areas for breakfast and lunch, and a theater with a Vegas-type stage. The ten decks, he told me, had about two thousand rooms.

"Mr. Evans buys used cruise ships, refurbishes them, adapts one side for coupling to the operations barge, then adds extra communications gear and unidirectional propellers underneath. It's more cost-effective than buying new."

"How many people in the crew?" I asked.

"Seventy-three. Thirty operate the ship, and the others run the platform. We have a regular rotation schedule like offshore oil rigs. Four weeks on, two weeks off, and regular vacations. We have a social director on board for planning games, entertainment, stage shows, that sort of thing. Each crew member has full use of the pool, hot tubs, entertainment areas, and exercise room."

"He uses a cruise ship with ten decks and two thousand rooms to house a crew of seventy-three?"

Van Thiem nodded and smiled courteously. "Yes. The ships we buy come with all the automated seaworthiness of a standard ocean-going vessel, plus all the utilities, storage, food service, communications, and everything else we need. Buying used ships makes them cost-effective. When crew members come back from leave, we assign them different cabins, so all two thousand cabins are used in the two years before the ship goes in for refurbishing, making it feel clean and efficient without wasting resources. When you see the barge, you'll appreciate the importance of having a vessel this large as part of the platform."

We passed through a seven-deck atrium complete with a glass-enclosed elevator and a sweeping stairway, and came to a set of polished wood double doors with a badge reader. Parker's suite was built out of two decks' worth of cabins directly below the operations and control center and the ship's bridge, giving him spacious quarters and rooms to host corporate meetings with all the trappings of an executive suite. Van Thiem waved his ID card across a plate, a click responded, and he pulled open one of the doors.

I walked into a palace. The room had a tall ceiling, several sofas, chairs, TV monitors, glass cases of shipwreck relics and nautical memorabilia, and three or four large displays of museum-quality wooden ship models, with paneled walls hung full of engineering drawings describing every aspect of the trash processing complex. Everything gleamed with polish and new upholstery, and looked every square inch of rich.

We crossed into another room with a meeting table big enough for twenty, plus a corner bar, and into a smaller office suite, three rooms with desks, a variety of computers and monitors, chairs, and floor-to-ceiling bookcases, all fronting an open door to a large private office—which was empty.

"He must be upstairs in his library."

Going farther into a foyer surrounded by perfectly cleaned glass windows overlooking the ship's bow, we walked up a sweeping staircase to a set of thick hand-carved teak double doors, opened them, and found another hallway with several closed doors. Van Thiem knocked on the first door, and Parker Evans opened it.

He looked at me with a broad smile of perfect, glistening white teeth. "Damn, Jack, you're really looking old."

"Well, Parker, you're even shorter than you look on TV," I said, grinning back at him.

He laughed, shook my hand, thanked Van Thiem, and we walked into his inner sanctum.

"This looks like a hideout," I said. The room was jammed with bookcases full of jumbles of books, magazines strewn around the floor, and two large easy chairs in the center, a light over each, buttressed with more piles of books.

"Thanks," Parker said. "I did the decorating myself. It's where I hide when my board of directors comes for a meeting."

He pointed me to the second chair and we sat, much as we'd done at his house before he poisoned his hamster. He did actually appear shorter than I remembered, with slightly wavy, tousled, gray-blond hair, but he was trim, looked fit, and was pretty damned handsome. Maybe he had bought some of it—a tummy tuck or some Botox—but he looked remarkably close to what I remembered from seeing him in the media. His shirt was a Jimmy Buffett-style mix of island colors, and he wore light cotton cargo pants, the same as Van Thiem. It must be the uniform of the ship's upper echelon, I thought.

We still looked like Mutt and Jeff. My years of football had removed the chunkiness of adolescence, and I thought I'd maintained a relatively trim shape, considering it was now some forty years later. I hadn't lost my height, either, and towered over him.

"You're as tall as I remember, but I see you use a donut diet to keep your muscles sleek and hide your wrinkles," Parker said with a smirk.

"Hey, I only eat the little ones without sprinkles. As for the wrinkles, remember that we're the same age, although I have to admit you look just a tiny bit younger."

"Maybe a tiny twenty years younger," he said as his tan glowed in the sunlight from the window. "Of course, you have to remember I'm a chemist, so I make my own versions of

Ambien, Prozac, Botox, Viagra, protein shakes, testosterone enhancers, wrinkle cream, and other never-get-old medicines. And you like my tan? Comes in a spray can, for which I've got the patent."

I laughed. "Maybe I should switch my prescription service to you."

We visited without really having much to say. He'd left before junior high, so he remembered almost no one from our youth and cared nothing about the local sports, honors, war heroes, bums, dropouts, divorces, deaths, or affairs that permeate the usual high school reunion.

We finally acknowledged the lack of small talk and began our grand tour of the ship, which I very much preferred. We retraced the way I'd come in, went up a couple of decks to a hallway of rooms that housed all the support functions— communications, weather, systems control, etc. and entered the ship's bridge. It looked as sophisticated as the deck of the *Enterprise*, with two long rows of consoles full of computer screens, buttons, circular handles, microphones, telephones, TV monitors, gauges, and more stuff I didn't recognize.

There were three people in the room, two of them scanning the sea with binoculars. The third stood with his arms crossed, looking down at a console.

"Who's steering the boat?" I asked mildly.

"It's done by satellite, if it's done at all. The platform drifts in a big circle with the current unless there's a reason to move it. If that happens, we have to have a certified captain on the bridge to go through starting the engines and monitoring the directions. Walk over here, and you'll get the royal view."

We passed the consoles and went out into a cantilevered viewing house that projected over the right side of the ship.

Wow! The squall was a dark shadow in the distance, letting the sunlight fully expose the massive complex below. I could see the full length of the cruise ship, the operations barge next to it, the systems of pipes, cables, pulleys, elevators, and other parts, and the immense—I mean, enormously immense—area that they call the lagoon.

"You know how all this works?" he asked.

I hadn't come down yet from being astounded by the sight. "Well, I read some articles, so I kind of know the principles. I didn't understand the details."

Parker pointed to a hundred or more tall monolithic structures off the side of the ship, bobbing up and down with the swells. They formed a ring, starting at one side of the barge below us and trailing far into the distance, then circling back, with a monolith every hundred feet or so along the rim. It all looked like an immense horse corral lit with blinking backyard tiki lights.

"The things sticking out of the water are big buoys connected to the filtration fabric," Parker told me. "That fabric is the heart of the facility. It's submerged right now, but we'll activate the buoys this afternoon, and they'll bring the fabric to the surface."

"It's an upside-down umbrella," I said, remembering my feeble attempts to understand how it all worked.

He laughed. "Yeah, well, okay, in a primitive sense. If you open an umbrella, turn it upside down, and take out the staves and handle, then when we pull it up, the fabric looks like an open umbrella with the fabric attached to cables around the outside."

He was describing a circular piece of fabric that's a thousand feet across with only the buoys around the edge to hold it up. I didn't know if he was automatically humble about the science or had lived with it long enough to be nonchalant. To me, it was as audacious as when I'd first read about it.

"Each buoy is the height of a four-story building," Parker said as he pointed to them. "Half is always below the surface, powered by unidirectional motors on the bottom, with gyroscopes and GPS units keeping it upright and in position. The half above the surface has the pulley mechanisms and motors that pull the cables up and let them down, and keep the skirt tight—that's what we call the filtration fabric: the skirt."

Twice each day, the buoys slowly let out the cables so that the skirt sinks. Then, even more slowly, to release the unpolluted sea water and small marine animals through the skirt's holes, the buoys winch the cables up, raising the skirt—my upside-down umbrella—so the seawater inside becomes a concentrated lagoon of *sludge* with the visible sea trash floating on top.

After that, everything floating on top is pushed to the processing barge by a wave action created by the buoys. "Dumping the lagoon," Parker said, "that's what we call getting all the trash and sludge out of the skirt."

On the barge itself, easily half the length of the ship, I could see the lagoon's exit port, the sweepers, the concentrator, the compactor, and several cranes at the far end. I was happy to see my now-famous Mexican sausages piled on the far end of the barge. Most would be packed with the sludge and small trash coming out of the concentrator and compactor, while the yellow-ended ones got big items loaded by the workers.

We went down from the ship, crossed the gangway above the grapples, and walked around the barge. The floor was going up and down with the swells much more than on the big ship, making it hard to walk; I didn't exactly have sea legs yet. Spray off the wave crests made it cold, and it all smelled awful.

"We pay a lot of attention to everything captured by the skirt, looking for objects that could damage it as it's brought up," Parker said. "There are dangerous things outside the lagoon as well. We put a lot of work into monitoring the sea around us, with binoculars, radar, sonar, and satellite. We've trained a couple of platform specialists to respond to anything in the water in the path of the platform.

"Whatever it is—like a capsized ship or a piece of a dock—it has to be either moved out of the way or sunk. We send out a big sea boat to inspect it, mark it, and if we can't sink it, we tow it around the platform.

"This facility is like a dead elephant floating in the water. We can't avoid anything, so whatever is in our path has to move."

CHAPTER 6

JAVIER C ADDED a new dimension to my thinking and another category to my homelessness assessment. He's technically homeless, but it's something he chose not because of the lack of money but as an economic strategy.

Javier is an adjunct professor of history at the big university here in town. Born to parents who'd escaped from Guatemala and settled in the US, he grew up as a citizen by birth. Unfortunately, his parents had entered the country illegally, and were both deported while he was in high school. His church arranged for him to live with a family until he turned eighteen and graduated. He enrolled at the university, got two degrees, and is now teaching a full load of undergraduate students. He is also recognized for his work with ESL students and the Latin American Culture Club.

Although a successful student, graduate student, and teacher, he finds himself still saddled with $50,000 in student loan debt.

Rent or mortgage payments would have taken most of his meager salary, with no way to significantly decrease his debt for years. Faced with those choices, Javier decided to spend the very minimum on his living accommodations and apply the money saved to pay down his student loans. He bought an old panel van and now lives in the parking lot next to the history building. A regular recreational vehicle is not allowed.

Living in a car or van is pretty common for the homeless. Vehicles are safer, offer more protection from the weather than any tent, and usually can be moved if something comes up. If you have access to a bathroom, a place to take a shower, and someplace to hang out beyond the four walls of your vehicle, it's not a bad situation.

Javier has all of those. As a university employee, the student center, cafeteria, gym, and other facilities are all available for his use.

Javier isn't a Streeter, technically speaking, but in reality, he's another casualty entrapped by the same economic system.

———————

JIM CRAMER, known for his TV show *Mad Money*, once lived in his Ford Fairmont for seven months.

Tyler Perry was sexually abused in a dysfunctional family and lived in his car while waiting to find success. Now he's one of the highest-paid performers in the entertainment industry.

William Shatner, one of the biggest celebrities in the world, slept in his covered pickup truck bed for months as the acting troupe he was part of went from city to city.

Steve Harvey wanted to be a comedian, and eventually became one of the most famous. Along the way, he lived in his Ford Tempo for three years, sleeping each night in the reclining front seat, showering and washing at gas station restrooms, pool showers, and hotel bathrooms.

CHAPTER 7

My tour with Parker was cut short when he was summoned to a conference call. I returned to my room, found snacks in the refrigerator, and spent the rest of the afternoon and early evening on the balcony, watching the barge and its expansive lagoon as it cycled through a full dumping. It was an agonizingly slow process. Everyone on the barge was busy for sure, but the skirt held hundreds of swimming pools' worth of water, sludge, and trash, and getting it all swallowed by the right receptacle on the barge required patience.

A couple of hours later, the towering buoys evened the level of the skirt and let it sink out of sight, where it would hang loose a hundred feet below the surface until sunrise when the buoys would slowly winch it up again.

Officially, the end of the afternoon dumping signaled supper time, even though it was almost eight at night. The barge operators secured the sausages, sprayed off their equipment and area, got things ready for the next morning, and then shut the barge down. Most people filed into the cafeteria for supper, dispersing afterwards for various activities. Along the deck walkway below my cabin, people headed to the pool or hot tubs, a few appeared covered with sweat from the exercise room, and a couple of men jogged around a track below me.

I put on shorts and a sports shirt, tried to look healthy and robust, and walked around the pool area, visiting. Everyone knew who I was and why I was there, and chatted me up like a favorite neighbor. My Mexico articles must have been required reading for the crew.

Most of the operating staff worked one of two shifts, from dawn until about one in the afternoon, and from then until sunset. That catches the two dumping cycles. The work had to be done in sunlight since so much depends on watching for items in the water. There were no breaks for meals, so the crew ate before and after their shifts, although food was available at any time from a refrigerator-based deli bar.

The ship's crew ran a more formal schedule. The bridge always needed at least three people: one spotter, who continually surveys the surrounding sea for anything that would be a danger to the facility, by sight and by monitoring radars and sonars; a weather person who stays in constant contact with the operations office in Hawaii and keeps a staff that keeps a constant eye on the weather; and a ship's officer who is responsible for the ship's operations and sea presence—where the facility is in relation to shipping channels, communicating with ocean traffic, and monitoring the ocean currents that carry the facility along. These positions require three eight-hour shifts through the day, with periodic breaks to relieve the tedium. They can eat whenever they want.

After visiting with the people at the pool and hot tubs, I went to the cafeteria. It had been built to serve hundreds, but only a small area was used so the crew could socialize more easily. I chatted informally, then isolated a few people for interviews. The international mix was readily apparent, and most seemed to be from Pacific Rim countries like Japan and South Korea, while others were from Europe, India, and

Brazil. Many had worked several years on regular cruise ships and had families back home. It's hard for me to imagine a full-time, year-round job in the middle of the ocean, but I guess it's no different from the life of most offshore workers.

As I'd found in Mexico, everyone was basically happy. The pay was excellent, the ship and its lagoon facility—the barge, buoys, and skirt—were all well-engineered, so minimal time was spent on repairs, and plenty of entertainment options were available. Wi-Fi helped fend off boredom, and pool parties, poker parties, birthday parties, and the like provided community get-togethers. Alcohol was casually available to anyone not on duty, but drunkenness was not tolerated.

If there was a common complaint, it was the isolation. And the wave motion. Both were something you got used to, but they could be wearing on the psyche if you spend a lot of time at sea. I could definitely understand it for those working on the barge, whose ups and downs were measured in feet.

According to Parker, given a good year of floating in the densest part of the Garbage Patch, plus all the time, money, and effort going into operating one platform came close to gathering a half percent of the estimated volume of loose trash and a tenth of a percent of the sludge. For an area twice the size of Texas, that ain't bad. Parker's corporation had twenty-one of the facilities around the world, and was looking to add a new one every year. It expected to always be in business as long as the world's countries continued polluting the oceans.

Whatever the numbers, Parker had effectively addressed a global calamity, and it won him his second Nobel Prize—the Peace Prize.

Pretty damn impressive.

After doing my evening's quota of interviews, I watched the cooks—who looked Italian—and servers clean up, then sat in the seven-story atrium area, looking at the empty chairs around me. After being so caught up in the activities all day, it was hard to be alone, so I went back to my room to think about my yet-to-be-started articles. It had been a no-surprises day of seeing an operation that was brutally efficient, minimally controlled, and clicking right along with everybody as happy as a clam.

Which means it wasn't.

Don't call me a cynic, call me a realist. My gut was telling me everything can't be fine, because people aren't made that way. Out in the middle of the ocean for weeks and months at a time? Nah, something bad had to be happening; I just couldn't see it. I'd worked the big city street beat for over twenty years, and I knew there was always something going on. One person scamming another, someone cheating on someone else, or being a pharmacy for a slew of needy customers. I knew people who'd shoot off a few pistol rounds at their neighbors just because they were bored. There's not an ocean-based oil rig in the world that doesn't have a jail cell tucked away somewhere below decks—not for criminals, mind you, but just for the ordinary human variations in employee behavior.

I felt sure I was missing something—and that's when Molly Sanger walked over and introduced herself. She came up to me at breakfast the next morning, telling me her name and pointing to the ID card hanging around her neck. She sat down and visited in a friendly manner, asking about how I found the operations, if I thought the food was good, and other small talk.

She was nice, I was nice, I made a few notes. She was a weather forecaster, working on the staff of one of the three officers on the bridge. She had been onboard a month.

She was a graduate research assistant when she saw the job ad. It was a chance to do something different, yet important, and a ton of money more than what other graduates in the real workforce were making. She could also use her off time for online courses toward a master's degree. Eventually, she hoped to make enough money to take a year off and go to the Galapagos, Peru, and maybe even the Arctic.

I immediately liked her. She seemed happy, easy-going, relaxed, and welcoming. I noticed only casually when she slipped a note into my pad of paper while reaching for the salt. Soon, she said goodbye and went back to her room to do an online class.

I waited until I was back in my room to read the note. Its first sentence was a warning: The wristband's microphone was always on, which meant everything I said or anyone else said could be heard by someone listening in, and the tracking disk worked whenever it was queried, so they could know where I was whenever they wanted.

Personally, I'd been thankful for my electronic handcuff, and found it rather humorous that it was the one object everyone had in common besides their nametags. It was like a gang sign tattooed on everybody's wrist. I hadn't taken seriously what Van Thiem had said about its usefulness if I ever fell off the ship, but looking over the railing at the ocean had brought back every story I'd read about cruise ship passengers falling overboard. A person could be dressed in neon yellow and still be only a small reflection against the color palette of the sea. With all the trash bobbing in the water around us, there was zero chance of being noticed.

As to the wristband being a tracking device, I found it amusing to think of myself as a slowly moving—or not—green dot on some electronic console, revealing my getting up to pee at night, my happy hour visits to the bar, and even my time in front of the slot machines.

I had told myself that it didn't matter and I shouldn't care. I wasn't going to be there that long, it was a big ship, and it was their ship. They must have good reasons for knowing where everyone was whenever they wanted to know. But having the microphone turned on continuously? That was a load of crap. My conversations with people had nothing to do with safety, and should be of no concern to anyone else.

In addition to the warning about the microphone and the tracking, Molly's note also said there were cameras everywhere that monitored every square inch of the ship, continuously, especially in the social areas, like the cafeteria where we'd met. There were no cameras in the cabins or the bathrooms, the note said. If we could deafen our wristbands, the two of us could talk privately in a cabin, which was what the rest of her note asked for. She needed to talk with me as soon as possible. She had found something going on that didn't make sense.

She couldn't tell anyone in the crew, so I was her only safe listener—though maybe it was nothing, she added.

Her work shift was from ten at night to six in the morning. She would come to my cabin after midnight, during her first thirty-minute break. I was to take off my wristband and leave it under the covers of my bed, making Big Brother think I was asleep while we talked in the bathroom.

I was surprisingly anxious, but this is what reporters like me live for. In the midst of Happy Ship, USA, had she found a crack in the facade? What had Molly seen that was so suspiciously unusual? Why couldn't she talk to anyone else about it? Did she feel threatened?

And cameras everywhere? Sure, if you had a few thousand people and a hundred crew members to watch a thousand monitors. But for a crew of a little more than seventy fully dedicated to their work, with locators on their wrists, it felt suspiciously like someone was expecting crimes to be committed. Did the bosses not trust the crew to keep their wristbands on? Did they want to catch anyone who didn't? Or was there something secret going on?

I did interviews during the rest of the day, dozed by the pool, then opened my cabin door at the set time that night. No one was in the hallway. Suddenly, the woman I'd met at breakfast appeared and slipped in the door, quietly closing it behind her. She must have practiced slipping around the hallway cameras.

But as the door closed and I looked into her eyes, she wasn't invisible—she was frightened.

"Something strange is happening at night," Molly whispered as we disappeared into the spacious tub area and closed the door.

The weather monitoring room in which she worked was part of the complex I had walked through on the way to the bridge. Since she was constantly updating the forecasts for the first officer, she had the combination to the bridge doors. It was during her first week, on the night shift about two in the morning, when she first noticed something unusual. The forecast was quiet for several hours out, and she'd taken a few minutes to wander the upper decks and acquaint herself with the ship's layout.

She had unexpectedly entered the bridge from the outside door.

"The first officer was focused on a monitor showing a smaller ship backing up to the stern of the cruise ship. It was a freighter—a utility ship with large, flat deck doors and cranes for moving cargo in and out of the holds—and it was slowly pulling up to the big, open supply doors while ropes were being readied to tie it onto the bigger ship."

No lights, no horns from either ship, no radio chatter. Even a novice would recognize this wasn't protocol—nothing happens on a big ship at night without floodlights illuminating the deck.

The first officer hadn't noticed her come up from behind, but when he did, he immediately asked her to leave, even pushing her into the hallway. Again, even to a novice, it seemed clear that treatment of that kind should never happen. It made her feel strange, as well as curious, so at her next break, she left her wristband behind the toilet in a nearby bathroom and slipped to the back of the ship to see if the mysterious freighter was still there.

She didn't make it very far. The lower parts of the ship—the engine room, the dispensary, the vast empty rooms that typically store equipment and supplies for a cruise, the waste disposal system, and the long access hallway used to distribute materials throughout the *Sea Sweep*—were all locked or blocked off. The crew was allowed in every part of the ship during the day, so why were the same areas locked at night?

The passageways on the top decks were cordoned off by rolling steel gates. Knowing she was due back at her post in a few minutes, Molly climbed over the barriers to the upper deck and looked over at the waters off the stern. Peering into the darkness, she barely made out the unlit freighter separating from the ship. Its lights remained off as it chugged into the distance.

She hurried back to her station.

In the following days, Molly used her break times to sneak to the back of the ship and look for the freighter—it had been back twice. Something was being secretly loaded or unloaded on a regular basis.

I listened but drew no conclusions. I've been in situations before where people grumbled with discontent and would purposefully make stuff up, partly from a need for drama but sometimes out of needless fear or touches of paranoia. Molly didn't fit that pattern. She talked quickly and well, though obviously suspicious that something bad was going on. She'd come to no conclusions as to what it was but assumed that she'd stumbled across something sensitive and covert. Maybe it was because she was stuck on a ship with no way to flee that she was afraid to talk to other crew members or ask the officers outright. That left me as the only choice she had.

"It's coming tonight," Molly said. "That's why I had to tell you as soon as possible. I compared satellite images over the last month. The freighter comes every three or four days. It starts from San Francisco, comes directly here, then goes straight back. It left San Francisco yesterday on the same bearing."

A shiver ran up my spine. But even if there's a mysterious ship, it doesn't mean that something evil or sinister is taking place. Maybe Parker's doing research he can't do in daylight, maybe he's got a special team doing something he wants to keep private, maybe the mysterious ship is full of auditors who demand ninja-type approaches—I've met auditors like that, so don't laugh—or, most likely, the visiting ship contained dignitaries from nations that wanted clandestine meetings with no publicity.

I wanted to talk more, but Molly got up and slipped out the door. She was invisible again.

I wished we had had more time.

CHAPTER 8

RANDY D ADDED yet another category to my list of street people: He was the kind of guy you hoped someone would hit with a truck. I had seen him on several corners, which is unusual for the typical Streeter. He also stood or sat with his sign a few feet from other panhandlers at the same intersection, and I'd seen him race to the open window of a car more than once while blocking the other person's path. That's a violation of the street code: No one ever invades someone else's territory, and you certainly don't horn in on anybody else's take.

I figured his story would be different from the others. He demanded that the interview take place behind a big thrift store. In the alley. Alone. Which made me think his interest was mostly in my wallet. No dice, I told him. It had to be out in the open, or not at all.

Chuckling as if he'd just been joking about the alley, we sat on a bench outside an Albertson's.

"Do I get paid for this?" he asked.

"No."

"Why the hell should I do it?"

"I asked, you said yes. If you don't want to, walk away."

"Ah, hell, maybe I'll be famous," he said.

Randy had grown up as the middle child in a lower-middle-class family. He'd been a solid *B* student in high school, played football and basketball and was pretty good at both, had a steady girlfriend, fixed up an old Chevy to drive, and had a normal circle of friends. He decided to be a SEAL, so he joined the Navy right out of high school.

Randy made it through the Navy's basic training but quickly flunked out of SEAL school, which left him bitter and resentful, claiming that the SEAL training was an excuse for egomaniacs to abuse people. He managed a transfer to the Army infantry, which he liked better, and served two tours in Afghanistan. He was on routine patrol through an Afghan village when his Humvee hit an IED, rolling the men inside and bashing body parts against metal. His lower leg snapped in half.

He was repaired and sent back to the states, where he recovered with the help of a lot of drugs and a lot of time spent doing nothing. He couldn't get his mind straight about whether he had been a hero or a fool. Either way, his bitterness grew and he became a hater of Muslims, a hater of the military, and eventually a hater of all things *not* Randy. By the time his body had healed, the drugs had become something he couldn't do without.

After his discharge, he bummed around, sleeping on friends' sofas and crisscrossing the country by thumb. He finally decided his future was in the drug trade. Already hooked on opioids, he moved up to cocaine and heroin, and after using them for a while, became a dealer in whatever people were willing to buy. He eventually left his home town of Detroit for the Southwest's warmer winters, and set himself up as a low-level supplier to low-level users.

He's a mean man—drug dependent, feeling persecuted and entitled at the same time, and blaming others for his problems. Homeless and bitter, he's the street thug who others actively avoid. He might find a warm bed with a woman for a while but then leaves when she wants him to help with expenses. Then it's back to sofas or old mattresses in rundown buildings, or squatting in empty houses that have been abandoned or are waiting to be sold.

Randy doesn't like anyone. He invades street corners with pleading signs, pushing out the smaller panhandlers—he's a big guy—and is not beneath roughing up the next guy for his measly amounts of change. His sign will tell you he's a homeless, jobless, wounded veteran, down on his luck—God Bless! He's known for shoplifting at Walmarts, liquor stores, and QuikStops, and views any token jail time as a vacation.

"Why don't you go to a trade school?" I asked. "You could do okay in construction or plumbing or something like that."

"Why would I do that? You get a real job, and there's always someone out to screw you. To hell with them. I might get me a job in a chop shop someday, 'cause I'm good with my hands and all, but I've got time. I'm in no hurry."

"You like being on the streets?"

"Hell, yeah. It's an adventure. I'm free to do what I want. I'm not like the other lowlifes around here. Bunch of losers. I can be a normal person anytime I want, but I got good connections to suppliers and users that are anxious to pay, so, hell, why change now? I even gave myself a bonus last year. Took a cruise with a Bahama Mamma."

Which means Randy's also a liar. If he's got good connections in the drug trade and makes enough money to give himself a bonus, why is he begging on the streets at all? Probably, I suspect, he burns far more money on his own habit than he's willing to admit, and keeps coming back to the street because it's easy and lets him get by with a minimum of effort. It's not hard to think that his success in the drug business is mostly a well-maintained delusion.

"You have trouble being hooked on your product?"

He laughed. "Hooked? Hooked? You are such an asshole. You're only hooked if you don't have any. You think I've got a drug *problem*? Hell, I've got a drug *solution!*" Randy laughed even more.

"What about your family?"

"My family can kiss my rosy red ass. All they want is my money, which I ain't gonna give them. My ex-wife thinks just because she's got the kid that I'm supposed to take care of her. Fat chance on that. To hell with her. Let her get a better job if she needs more money. My parents are the same way. Why the hell should I give them money? I've got my own life to live, and if they don't like being poor, it's because they earned it. Should've saved their money, right? Go to a home or something, get on welfare. Shit, I'm busy with my own life now."

"What about the future? Do you have any plans?"

"You think plans are everything, right? You gotta have plans so you can get ahead in life, be successful, kiss some boss's ass so you can be a slave to some shithead until you make enough to retire. I'm doing my living right now. Screw the rest of you. I'm moving up just like I want to, and I'll have me a big house and a fancy car soon enough. I've got women like you wouldn't believe. Every woman I know wants me, so I'll just put in a conveyor belt and let them all have a lick. Shit, hell, I'm on my way. You screw off."

That was enough for him and he left.

It was enough for me, too.

———

HOMELESSNESS AMONG UNITED STATES veterans cuts across demographics. On any given night, an estimated forty thousand veterans are homeless, with an estimated 1.4 million other veterans at risk of becoming homeless because of their substandard housing, poverty, and lack of support from family or social networks. More than forty thousand homeless vets receive some type of compensation or pension benefits.

Veterans have twice the risk of becoming chronically homeless as other Americans. There are more homeless veterans from the Vietnam era than soldiers who died fighting in the war.

Homelessness affects both male and female veterans, with women representing about 8 percent of homeless US vets. All age groups are represented, but more than forty percent range from ages thirty-one to fifty. Among homeless veterans, some fifty-one percent have disabilities, fifty percent have a serious mental illness, and seventy percent have substance abuse problems.

CHAPTER 9

IF THE MYSTERIOUS freighter was mating up with the big ship tonight, I had only an hour or so to get myself out the door. Not that I was convinced something improper or illegal was going on, but if there was, I wanted a front-row seat.

Maybe.

The honest truth was that I had anticipated spending some downtime lounging in a chair next to the pool, relieving some of the tensions earned by pumping out words under deadlines. If I was going to get myself involved in snooping around, justified or not, I could kiss the relaxed cruise idea goodbye. Yes, I'm a reporter, and yes, I'm supposed to pursue truth and investigate suspicious behavior like a true crimefighter, but this was Parker, my childhood friend, and I was his guest. How about if I just have a great night's sleep instead of spending the time chasing ghost ships? Was I really going to take his kind invitation and use it to prowl around his ship? Isn't that rude? I mean, this is Parker Evans, Nobel Prize winner. I doubt he would have invited me aboard at the same time he was doing something nasty.

Maybe somebody else was orchestrating the nighttime freighter hookup, and Parker didn't know about it. Van

Thiem was in a perfect position to hide things from his boss, or maybe it was the captain.

But even so, why did it have to be me that catches them? Why couldn't Molly figure it out?

Well, yeah, but what's the point of being a respected newspaperman if you're not going to investigate a mysterious activity? Maybe I'd find something else for my not-yet-given-up-on book about Parker. Or was it that my career was slowly slipping into the geriatric realm? Was it time to sit on a park bench and take up whittling toothpicks?

Well, okay, I'd check it out. But I was definitely going to sleep late tomorrow.

It was one-thirty when I slipped out into the hallway and took the stairs to the upper deck. No lights were on, so I assumed it wouldn't matter if there were cameras. I considered the idea I was being watched pretty silly anyway. Who would spend their time staring at a bunch of screens all the time?

I found one of the steel gates Molly had talked about. I struggled over it in the clumsiest of fashions, hoping no camera was watching. I had visions of it showing up on *America's Funniest Home Videos*. I went through the service doors used to bring food to the swimming pool area and then took a back stairway down several decks, looking for the large service corridor that ran below the passenger decks. It was the major artery for moving things in and out of the ship's storage rooms. If anything was being offloaded from the visiting freighter, that's the way they'd go.

At the bottom of the stairs, I turned toward the stern and went carefully down a hall that curved around to a set of locked double doors. I told you I'd worked the police beat back home. Cops are always wanting to impress anyone riding along with them, so I learned all sorts of tricks, including using a knife blade for jimmying a door lock.

Cautiously slipping through the door, I stepped into the main passageway I was looking for. The corridor was wide and empty and absolutely dark, but at the far end, two sets of tall doors opened into well-lit rooms, each on opposite sides of the corridor. As I slipped along the side of the corridor, a man in a hazmat suit came into view, driving a forklift. Another man, also in a hazmat suit, came from inside the room opposite me, and moved to work at a control panel near the stern.

Suddenly, large overhead lights came on and lit the back wall as a good part of it began to open and swing away. I ducked behind a bulkhead and squatted down in the shadows.

Two massive doors cranked open like a bomb bay. Caught in the overhead light, a smaller ship began backing up to the opening as I watched. The operator parked the forklift, got down, and positioned himself to help the ship tie up.

It didn't look easy as the small ship rocked and swayed while waves pounded it from the side, the swells moving it up and down in front of the opening. A couple of crewmen on the freighter threw ropes over to the big ship, the operator sliding them around large posts. A narrow metal ramp was extended over the gap between the ships and anchored on both ends. Now secured, the freighter settled into the rhythm of the larger ship, and a set of cargo doors on its deck opened up. Unhooking a crane from a pole in the center, the crew lifted a large rectangular container, maybe eight feet by four feet by four feet, out of the hold and moved it over to the floor of the bigger ship. The operator had retaken the seat on the forklift, started it up, slid its tines underneath, lifted, and shuttled the container into the room on my left.

Less than a minute later, the forklift returned carrying an identical container. It could have been the same one, except that it rocked back and forth on the tines as the forklift turned, reversed, and moved forward. Seeing the container slide and wobble as it was hooked to the crane's slings and swung quickly over to the freighter, I guessed it was empty. After lowering that one, another container soon appeared out of the hold and was moved to the forklift. They must be exchanging full containers for empty ones, I figured—but full of what, empty of what? The containers didn't look like any shipping crates I'd ever seen.

Peering from behind the bulkhead into the room across the corridor, I could see a complex combination of mechanical structures, ten or twelve feet high, fronted by a conveyor belt, walkways, lifts, and large waist-high aluminum surfaces. On the other side of the structures was the dark shape of a single, smaller version of the sausages used on the barge, its end slanting upward and hooked onto a large chute.

I had heard all sorts of grinding, pumping, and ratcheting sounds coming from the room, but it went quiet as the forklift began the exchange of containers.

After the last empty container, the operator helped disconnect the smaller ship. I had counted thirty containers taken off the freighter and another thirty loaded onto it. It had taken more than two hours, and my legs were killing me from crouching in my hiding place. The ramp between the two ships was pulled back, the connecting ropes were undone, and the freighter chugged away as the huge clamshell doors swung closed. The overhead lights turned off, leaving me once again in the semi-darkness of the corridor. I stood and stretched my legs, relieved I had witnessed the operations without being exposed.

The second man in a hazmat suit, the one who had come out of the far room to run the controls, returned inside the room, while the forklift operator climbed back on his machine, swung it around, and retrieved a single container from the storage room, taking it into the mechanical room across the corridor. The noise from the room began again, and a number of minutes, twenty-five or thirty, I guessed, elapsed before the forklift backed out of the mechanical room with the container, turned around and deposited it into the storage room. I presumed it was now empty and that the room with all the structures was where the emptying of the containers was taking place.

No spoken words, no wasted movements, no hesitation. The two men certainly knew their routines, but why were they wearing hazmat suits? Any kind of germ danger on a ship at sea was a major threat, but having an operation that deliberately involved hazardous materials was crazy.

While the forklift was busy fetching another container, I crossed the corridor and slipped behind the open door of the mechanical room. Looking back at where I had come, I had a clear view of the storage room and did a quick count—thirty-one, maybe thirty-two containers. If Molly had the freighter showing up every three or four days, it must take that long to get them all emptied, plus or minus a few, for whatever Parker was doing with the contents. The operation certainly was not trivial, and my imagination was beginning to run wild. What in the world could be inside the containers?

Hoping to find out, I had snuggled up behind the mechanical room door to peer through the opening between the hinges when Parker Evans walked up behind me and asked if I would like to go inside.

————

HE WAS NOT HAPPY.

"Even a newspaperman should have limits on his curiosity," he said, "and this is a good example. I didn't invite you to visit so you could go snooping around the ship."

I was pissed and embarrassed, both from looking like an amateur tourist playing Sherlock Holmes and from the fact that my movements obviously had been observed. In spite of the fact that I *was* snooping, I still resented Big Brother's watching. They couldn't have located me by my wristband, since it was still under the covers back in my room, so it must have been hallway cameras or maybe night-vision ones hidden in the corridor. I wasn't sure, but it didn't seem like the cameras were such an innocent activity anymore.

Van Thiem, who had come up behind Parker on his catch-the-criminal moment, handed each of us a set of ear protectors, and we stood for a moment on the threshold of the room with the intricate machinery. There were two workers inside, both wearing hazmat suits, and with the operator of the forklift, that made three for the whole business.

Whatever they were doing, and for whatever reason the suits were needed, everything inside this room was being kept secret from the rest of the ship.

Compared with what I had only peeked at, the mechanical room was a large space with steel walkways and stairs weaving in and out, cranes and pulleys hanging from large I-beams across the ceiling, industrial lights, and a small control room full of monitors. At waist level to my left, a wide aluminum table with foot-high sides sat directly under a raised shelf on which one of the containers from the storage room had been opened and tipped on its side. White sacks that must have been inside lay spilled across a table, each one seven or so feet long, relatively flat like an envelope but with large lumps here and there.

The forklift moved beside a panel, and the operator pulled a lever down. The empty container above him slowly lowered onto the forklift, and the man returned it to the room across the hall.

The worker at the lower table shuffled the bags so that two nozzles attached to each were pointing outward. He positioned them end-to-end as he fed them onto the conveyor belt. As each bag crept up to the next level, it was pulled across an upper table by the third man. After connecting a hose onto one of the nozzles, he pulled a lever up and down, disconnected the hose, threaded a cap onto the nozzle, then sent the sack sliding down the inclined chute into the small sausage I had seen. The tube was maybe a third as long as those on the barge and two-thirds the diameter. I could see that it was at least half full, the sides of the sausage distended and bumpy near the bottom.

I had immediately recognized the sacks spilled from the container: They were body bags. I'd seen a lot of body bags in my career: The end-to-end zippers and handles on the corners made them easy to identify, but the nozzles were something I hadn't seen before.

"What the hell are you doing?" I shouted over the noise.

Parker gave a grimace and led me up a stairway into the glass-enclosed control room. Van Thiem followed, unobtrusively but at-the-ready for anything Parker would want. When he closed the door, the noise was muffled, and we took off our ear protection to talk.

"There's a long history," Parker began, "but I'll give you the short version. Ebola containment and cleanup are big news today, and the World Health Organization is aggressively involved, but ten years ago, when epidemics in Africa were wiping out thousands of people, anybody with half a brain could see that disposing of infected bodies was going to be a problem. They tried burying them, but people complained about contaminating the soil. They tried piling them up and burning them, but the smoke and ash went everywhere, and people feared it would spread the disease through the air. No one had a solution, and they asked me to help."

He looked me in the eye. "I only provided them a service, that's all. I brought them a ton of body bags, had them loaded with the infected bodies, and took them out to a platform in the South Atlantic. I made special tubes that were mechanically and biologically secure, put the body bags inside, sealed each tube, put weights on them, and slid them into the ocean. Sitting on the bottom of the ocean, they're absolutely safe, with no danger of contaminating anything. The tubes are secure forever.

"It was a viable solution for all concerned, so I processed all the bodies they had, and we parted ways. A few months later, two new countries showed up with their own truckloads of bodies. Famine had killed them. I repeated the operation. Then some despot I don't want to name who'd killed thousands in a bloodbath of a civil war contacted me. He didn't want to bury the bodies because the country needed every inch of farmland it could get, and he didn't want anyone digging up the bones accidentally. I suspect he also didn't want to leave any evidence around. He offered me a lot of money, which made me realize that disposing of unwanted bodies might be a viable business. I modified a couple of my ocean platforms and began offering bagging and sinking as a regular solution when international crises turned up."

I watched the bags working their way up the conveyor belt onto the table at the top. Each one had a barcode.

"Why the barcodes?" I asked. "You plan on retrieving them someday?"

"Let me finish my story, Mr. Snooper," Parker replied, clearly irritated. "I still respond to emergencies like disease breakouts or famines, and I charge for it, but it made me realize the need for disposing of unclaimed bodies from city morgues and mortuary schools around the country. After seeing the numbers, I developed a domestic side to the business to dispose of these unclaimed bodies, and it's worked pretty well. That's the only business we do on this platform. The barcodes are put there by the bag manufacturer as part of their bookkeeping. We couldn't care less about the barcodes because where these bodies are going, they'll never, ever be retrieved."

Van Thiem passed him a paper with a column of names. Parker handed it to me.

"It's expensive for cities to handle the bodies of the vagrants who die there. Or whose families can't afford to bury their relatives. Or bodies of immigrants whose families no one knows. Sometimes, in big cities, every nook and cranny of the morgue is filled with bodies waiting to be disposed of. Sometimes, they're donated to medical schools and mortuary training, but the city has to dispose of the rest.

"In an average year, America has a hundred thousand unclaimed bodies. That means it's costing the country millions of dollars to either bury or cremate bodies pulled out of deserted buildings or found in ditches or discovered who knows where, and that's after keeping them preserved for six months, waiting for them to be claimed.

"If the bodies are cremated, that's hundreds of pounds of cremated remains fouling up the ground. If they're buried, that's millions of pounds of decaying flesh rotting in cemeteries. It's not like they use high-dollar coffins, so it's not long before the caskets disintegrate and those bodies become part of the dirt. That list shows seventeen cities we service on a regular basis. Each one of them is saving money and real estate every time they send me a body.

"Last year, I disposed of ten thousand bodies, putting them in a place that has infinite capacity, will never be seen, and is environmentally safe. That's a lot of positive impact on the environment."

He pointed to a monitor on the wall above our heads. "The ocean floor is about a mile below us, so the tubes we fill drop like rocks straight to the bottom, where they'll stay for the rest of eternity. It's a hell of a lot better than putting bodies into the ground and letting the earthworms spread their bacteria into the water table.

"And you know what?"

I looked at him. He was way too casual about the whole business.

"What?"

Parker smiled. "This part of the business, the domestic part, I do for free. The whole thing—bags, bodies, trucks, freighter, processing—all of it doesn't cost America a dime."

I watched out the control room windows as the men worked. One body bag after another traveling from container to tube.

"We treat all the bodies like they're diseased because, well, maybe they are. Some of them have been autopsied, some not, and some that we get from mortuary schools are even embalmed, but we can't be sure, so that's why the crew wears hazmat suits. They never open the body bags, but it's a guard against a bag accidentally getting ripped or something. And the crewman up there," Parker pointed to a man at the upper table, "he's squirting disinfectant into every bag. That's a little overkill to me, but it's a good business practice. I don't want anyone accusing me of poisoning the ocean with bacterial diseases. All the bags are put in these special tubes, the tubes are sealed, and as they sink, they're crushed by the water pressure. That second port on the bag is a pressure relief valve, and I've got one on the tube as well. As everything sinks, all the air is squeezed out, and the bags end up crushed like wadded-up newspapers."

More bodies kept sliding down the chute, and the conveyor belt kept on cranking.

I tilted my head and looked at him. "You mean you spend billions getting plastic out of the ocean, and then you use plastic bags to sink bodies back in it?"

He gave a small smile. "I love the irony, don't you?"

Parker pointed at the paper in my hand.

"That list is for the United States," he said as he looked at me. "Treating bodies this way has turned into a successful and effective business, and is certainly improving the environment and the economy, so I'm shopping it around to other countries because it's got to help with different cultures, too. Put yourself in the government of any one of those countries and tell me what you would do when you've got hundreds of people dying every day. Political leaders used to worry about body counts, but now they worry about square footage.

"Take India, for example. Go to Mumbai. There are some parts of the city that have a million people in a ten-block radius. It's so crowded that if you die, you don't even have room to fall over. You know what they used to do with their dead? Threw them in the Ganges. My God, can you imagine being in a boat when your propeller starts shredding some-body's grandmother? They finally stopped, but now they burn everything in funeral pyres on the shore. All those partially burned flakes of bodies going up in the air, where do they go? Into the river where people are bathing and washing clothes, unless they float over the city and cake everything in ash. I'm trying to convince them there's a better way."

I didn't know what to say. Honestly. Disposing of the dead was one aspect of earth management I hadn't even remotely considered. In America, we do all we can so that human bodies *never* disintegrate—fill them full of formaldehyde, put them in high-dollar protective coffins, put the coffins in concrete vaults, and bury them in land managed to last forever. We're antiseptic about it. If one cemetery fills up, we lay out another. Our crematoriums are even airtight, so from ashes to ashes is a healthy endeavor. You can keep Uncle Pete on the fireplace mantle if you want or add him to the flower beds in front of the house.

"My God, do you ever worry about being in this kind of business?" I asked.

Parker shrugged. "Does a mortician? It's easy to moralize and question your convictions about how you handle the dead, but if your country is a war zone where body parts are flying around and hundreds die every day, the effects on the environment of all those dead bodies is significant collateral damage. If it can be taken care of in a better and cleaner way, isn't that the logical and right thing to do?"

"How many people know you do this?" I asked.

He looked at me, then shrugged again. "I've never hidden the business, but I am discreet. Only the people who work here and the officers know about this business, but I don't hide it from anyone on the ship who asks. If it did go public? Bad publicity affects the supplier, not me. Societies don't like their government to be hard-hearted, and if it gets out that their elected officials are contracting for the wholesale disposal of their dead citizens, it might be a bad election year. Does your city back home broadcast what the morgue does? Does anyone care? Do they go out of their way to tell the public how many unidentified bodies they have laying around? Do my providers in Africa want people to know what they did?

"Jack, your problem is that you don't have a world view of things. There are real problems on this earth: real, genuine, global problems that require global solutions. It's our duty as citizens of the world to address them, and we shouldn't be squeamish about it. I think I've done something with the ocean cleaning business, and now I'm helping the world in other ways. Treating unwanted bodies is just another version of taking out the trash."

Van Thiem pointed at his watch.

"So now you've seen it, Mr. Snooper," Parker said as he prepared to put his ear protection back on. "I'm going to count on you to make sure news of this little operation never appears in your paper, or any other media outlet. We're patriots here, and we work for America. I need for you to be a patriot, too." He looked up at me, straight in the eyes, with a crooked smile. "And if you don't accept the responsibility, you may end up in one of those body bags."

We walked back into the noise, out the tall doorway and down the length of the corridor, listening to the echo of the conveyor belt as it delivered its next package of death to the tube. At the entry doors, Parker Evans turned left as Van Thiem turned me right.

Parker didn't bother saying goodnight.

At the door of my cabin, Van Thiem looked at me. "Don't take off your wrist band again. I'm not as nice as Mr. Evans," and walked away.

Closing the door after myself, I didn't know how to feel. I've gotten a lot of veiled threats in my life as a newspaperman, but Parker's really irritated me because it wasn't veiled at all. He had always been one to exaggerate his personal power, even in elementary school, so I'd learned not to pay any attention to his bullying. But the idea that I might end up in a body bag because I wasn't a good enough patriot really pissed me off. He could take his two Nobel prizes and shove them up his ass.

I was also still hot about getting caught, but the idea that I'd been let in on Parker Evans's secret did have an effect: I had been inducted into a covert international cooperative that few people on earth knew about. My asking if he worried about disposing of bodies as part of his work showed that I initially saw what he was doing as an issue of right or wrong. With his explanation, I was surprisingly relieved: It was neither right nor wrong but a service he had been called on to render at a time of great need. And from his description, it was a good service for the world to have. I wouldn't want to be a fisherman on the Ganges, nor washing my clothes in its waters.

I needed to find Molly and tell her what I'd found. It wasn't five in the morning yet, so she should still be at her desk in the weather monitoring room. My urgency to tell her everything made me realize I had crossed the line: I had accepted the body disposal operation as not only Parker's secret but also my own. I was ready to protect it.

I grabbed my wristband from under my covers, strapped it back on, and headed to the weather room, not caring if Big Brother was watching me or a green dot on a monitor. When I reached the room, a man was sitting in what was obviously the room's main chair, looking at several monitors of weather maps and data.

I was surprised. "Is Molly around?" I asked innocently.

"She wasn't feeling well and probably has a cold," he said. "Any kind of sickness is serious stuff on a ship at sea, so she's required to be confined to her room until the symptoms go away. It's pretty standard."

When he told me, the air went out of the room and I struggled to keep calm as I backed out the door.

That wasn't right. When she'd left my room not five hours ago, she had been fine. Had her clandestine visit to me been seen by one of the cameras? Had Parker and Van Thiem been aware of her prowling the ship during her breaks? Did they know she had seen the freighter in the night? Did they know what she had told me?

What would they do if they had?

CHAPTER 10

THE WORD GOT AROUND that I was talking to street people, gathering their stories. Often, those I interviewed pointed me to someone else for more information or a different perspective or a more horrific story. Most times, it didn't work out because finding one particular person in a widespread crowd of wanderers is tough. I still tried, even when I had more than enough material for my articles. I hated to miss another angle or new information that was unusual, more startling, or could give me a different insight.

Then something happened I thought I was way too experienced to fall into—I became obsessed with someone I interviewed.

I couldn't get her out of my dreams. It's always dangerous for a reporter to be sucked emotionally into their work because it can bias the reporting or mess with your mind if what you write doesn't get the reaction you hope for. Pouring yourself into a story and finding no one else cares about it like you do can be pretty devastating.

I make this preamble because Jamie E broke my heart.

Jamie E is eleven. She was sleeping on cardboard in back alleys when she was nine. That's the age of my grandkids, and

I worry about them spending an afternoon at the mall, much less sleeping a night next to an alley garbage bin.

Some of you reading this may have jumped immediately to the conclusion that I'm a slug or worse for not turning her in to some social organization, or the police, or not finding her a foster parent, or contacting a children's home instead of continuing with a dumb interview. She's way too young to be on the streets in any situation, and there are organizations and people who would gladly take her in a heartbeat.

I would have done those things, eagerly, but I had no idea where she was or who she was.

She refused to meet—she had heard about me, found my number, and called me. I don't know her real name, I don't know where she hangs out, I don't know what she looks like, or who her friends are, or even her neighborhood. Give me some slack here. I would have done the right thing if I could have.

Jamie was nine and her sister, Meg, was twelve when they ran away from home. Her father was a drunk and sexually abused both of them, while her mother was hooked on coke and heroin and selling her body to pay for them whenever she was conscious. After escaping the prison that was their home, the two girls hung out wherever they could, moved through a string of apartments and friends' houses, squatted if they could find an abandoned house or apartment, and lived in tent cities. Within a year of their leaving, their father went west, and their mother OD'd herself into the morgue.

What about school? *I been to a few. Can't go now because they want my parents to show up.*

What about your sister? *She took off with some guy a year ago.*

You have any kind of support? Money? Food? *I get caught if I show up alone at places, so I go to shelters and food lines and stuff* with my friends. *I can't go to no government places because they catch me.*

You have friends that care for you? *I live with three women right now. I ain't pretty but I can pass for older. They say I'm their daughter or niece, and it gets them more money. They give me some to buy things.*

Do you do drugs? *Nope. I seen my mom, and I don't want that.*

Wouldn't you want a family? Like to be adopted or something? There are organizations that would welcome you and take care of you. *Sometimes, I wish my sister would come back and we could be a family again, but I don't count on nobody sticking with me. I can't read good, so where are they gonna put me in school? Nobody wants a kid who's stupid.*

Where do you live? *Housing projects take single women with kids. That's where I'm staying now.*

Doesn't anyone notice you're alone? *I got a backpack, and I do up my hair and use the pack like I'm going to school, so nobody notices me.*

Are there things you wish for? *My teeth are messed up. I got slapped around when I was a kid and got some knocked out, and now everything's crooked. I try not to look in the mirror, but I can feel them when I talk and eat. I wish I could have a dog. We got a cat, but it don't like me. I wish I could read the words under the pictures in the books.*

Does anybody hurt you? *No answer.*

Sweetie, listen to me, okay, I've got an idea. Let me meet you at...

She hung up the phone.

———

In 2014, 45,205 children and youths were unaccompanied and on the streets, according to the annual point-in-time count of the Department of Housing and Urban Development.

About 80 percent of homeless youths, aged 12-21, use alcohol or other drugs as a way to self-medicate, to deal with a life of trauma and abuse. According to estimates by the Urban Institute, nearly one in five youths under the age of eighteen will run away at least once. Over 50 percent of young people in shelters and on the streets report that their parents told them to leave, or knew they were leaving and didn't care.

CHAPTER 11

I WOKE late in the morning to a different ship, one that felt unfamiliar—one that felt dangerous and unsafe, like a veil of secrecy had dropped over it.

That's the curse of being a good reporter: I'd worked hard on my interviews the first couple of days, and most of the articles had sort of written themselves after that. Things like structure, highlights, and an interesting, straightforward story basically flowed into place simply because I've been doing this for so long. I hadn't started to polish it yet, but I think it was pretty good.

But everything suddenly shifted. I had new information—major new information—and not using it would be cheating. I wanted to hold to my commitment to not reveal what I knew about Parker's business, but my resolve was crumbling. After all I had seen the night before, and with what Parker had told me, I couldn't sleep. I lay in the bed, going over and over what had happened, while the demons of doubt and suspicion pushed me to rethink every word that had come out of his mouth.

Why would a Nobel Prize-winning genius pick burying

bodies at sea as a clandestine business? He had made it sound noble, but come on, littering the sea floor with squished bodies? You don't franchise a zillion-dollar technology around the world and then create a side business you have to do in the middle of the night with guys in hazmat suits. And doing it for free? Why? Cities all over would be willing to pay, or at least share some of the costs.

Parker had never been shy about publicity, and here he could hold himself up as a model citizen of the planet, so why miss a chance like this?

And what was this patriot bullshit anyway? Since when was it patriotic to help out cities with their essential public duties? This was dumping bodies in the ocean, not taking care of used flags.

The biggest thing that kept me awake, though, was Molly suddenly becoming sick. My gut was telling me it was not true, and it had to be related to what happened last night.

Paranoia was creeping up my back, making me sweat. Despite what he had said, there was no way Parker would tolerate even a hint of exposure for his nighttime business. Not worried about people finding out? Freely telling anyone who asked? Being discreet? I don't think so. Even if it wasn't a moral question, the sheer volume of what he was doing would paint him as an ogre of first rank.

There's no way that littering the ocean floor with bodies wouldn't tick people off. He was way too casual about the possibility of people knowing what he was doing, which made me think he never expected the business to be discovered.

Which makes Molly look like a loose end—and makes me look like one, too.

In two days, I'd be leaving, and I wanted Molly on the chopper with me. But how to convince her? In fact, how was I going to even find her? I didn't know her room or phone number, and couldn't ask anything without the risk of being reported. I had to at least get her a message telling her what I had found. For all of the reasons that I shouldn't be suspicious of Parker and Van Thiem, I couldn't get past my feeling of danger.

Okay. That was the honest truth: She was scared, and now I'm scared.

Scared and tired, as if one wasn't enough. I'm used to eight or nine hours of sleep, and working on little or none had me wobbly on my feet. Investigative reporting was supposed to be James Bond-exciting and thrilling and absorbing. You never see any heroes losing sleep because of worry or fear; they don't even go to the bathroom. I am obviously not made for this kind of life.

But right now, I had to find Molly.

I got dressed and jogged downstairs. I questioned the cooks and the servers first. Maybe they were faking it, but none recalled Molly as I described her. There were few women on board and I expected any young, single, pretty woman would be memorable, but no one fessed up. I talked to the travel agent, the crewman who sorted the mail brought in each week, and the gift shop manager. No information there. Maybe Molly hadn't been on board long enough to need their services.

I talked to several of the people I had interviewed for my story, claiming a need to re-interview her. They all shook their heads. This was one disadvantage of an ethnically diverse workforce—they tended to know their own people and didn't necessarily pay attention to the others. Especially if they didn't speak the same language.

I ate lunch, carefully watching the people around me to see if their eyes had become shifty, or if they were avoiding looking directly at me. I looked around for the cameras that were surely watching me. I couldn't see any, but cameras these days can be made to look like anything.

I was freaking out. Parker said only the workers in the processing room and the officers knew of the body disposal activities, but it didn't make sense. You can't keep a secret in a community as tight as this one: Too many people talked, too many watched each other, too many wanted to know, too many would notice irregularities. How could it be that no one —no one?—had ever seen the freighter in the night?

I went back to the weather room upstairs. Nope, still haven't heard from her. Haven't heard if she's better or not. If she'd been quarantined, it would be for twenty-four hours.

Was everyone wearing a mask, or was it my imagination? Did they know? Had they been told not to answer my questions? Was it tied to the body dumping, or was it my questions that made everyone dumb? Was this the ultimate result of everyone wearing a microphone that was always on?

I retreated to my room, convinced I was being blocked. I paced back and forth, occasionally sitting, sometimes walking every square inch of the immense cabin, sometimes going out onto the balcony. Were there cameras on the balconies? I paced inside, again, back and forth, back and forth. The afternoon dumping had begun, and I glanced at the motions on the barge.

I finally sat down with a huff in the office chair, turned on the computer, and had a talk with myself.

- Is taking bodies from morgues and dumping them at sea bad or illegal? *No.*
- *Why does it feel bad? Secrecy, huge organization, other countries involved.*
- *Why does it seem good? Saves money, better environmentally.*
- *Is that perception? Maybe, but probably still true.*

- Is it because an operation that big can't be hidden? *Maybe.*
- Does it feel wrong? *Maybe.*
- Is it something this big as a front for something else going on? *Maybe.*
- Do I think that I'm being told the truth?

Parker had been upfront about things. He could have told me it wasn't any of my business, taken me back to my cabin, locked the door, and put me on the chopper the next day.

Of course, I'm a reporter who's writing a story about his ocean cleaning operations. He knew if he had escorted me off the ship, he could expect one of those *What's Really Going On?* articles the next week that would give him even more unwanted exposure.

Yeah. Okay. He couldn't *not* give me an explanation.

But he had invited me into the operations room and hadn't hesitated telling me the situation and answering my questions. The whole operation was plausible, and yes, even noble, and it all made good sense. Besides, there are other people involved. It's one thing to have a ship full of bad people, but everyone I'd met seemed nice and ordinary and showed no signs of working under a hard-ass organizational level of control. Maybe they all knew about it, maybe none of them knew about anything. Maybe it just wasn't a big deal for anyone.

Damn it! What was it that was bothering me?

Where's Molly? *Don't know.*

Is it because I can't find her that I'm freaking out? *Yes. Absolutely!*

If I had found her and we had talked and I'd told her everything, then I wouldn't be bouncing off the wall. It was her being nowhere and her apparent invisibility to the rest of the crew that was driving me nuts, as well as my lack of ability to look...

The wristband!

Dummy! Dummy! Dummy! Why didn't I think of that in the first place!

If I could see the wristband tracking information, I would know exactly where she was.

CHAPTER 12

Harold Plackery, Communications Technician.

I looked up his interview. He'd been with the facility for three years, is married with three kids, manages the four-weeks-on-two-weeks-off with ease. It's good money. He likes the assignment and is good at it. He'd been a technician with Comcast, then T-Mobile, then a private networking company for five years, and likes this a lot better.

He was on a break from his six o'clock morning shift when I'd interviewed him in the cafeteria, and I was hoping that pattern hadn't changed, because I was outside the communications room at one minute after six in the morning.

"Hey, Harold, how're you doing?"

He was sitting in his chair, surrounded by tall cabinets of electronic gear, blinking their lights at him, looking at screens of data. He's a good-looking guy, maybe in his early forties. As we were passing pleasantries, I slid him a note. I'd been afraid he might be the ears of the wristband microphone, but once I saw his setup, it didn't seem clandestine enough. If I were Parker, I'd have the eavesdropping stuff in my own office, or Van Thiem's, or someplace where no one could see me listening in on conversations.

I decided not to risk it, so I put my real question on paper. As I told him about the articles I was writing, he read my note: *Molly Sanger offered to give me a private tour of the hot tubs. Can you find her for me?*

He didn't flinch, slid his chair over to the front of another screen, typed in something, then toggled through a series of floor plans. He stopped on one that held a small blinking dot. He took my note, wrote the deck and cabin number on it, and smiled as he handed it back.

I wrapped up my conversation and left, wondering why I hadn't thought of this before.

———

"MOLLY! WHERE HAVE YOU BEEN?"

I knocked on the cabin door, she asked my name, then opened it with an expression of relief. There she was, standing in the doorway, hair in a mess, in pajamas—I had forgotten she'd be sleeping in the day because of her night shift schedule—as if it was perfectly normal, in her cabin like the guy in her chair had said. She wasn't chained, drugged, handcuffed, bopped on the head, or anything. I had it all wrong.

"I've been right here," she said as she invited me in. "All I did was sneeze once, and suddenly there were three people putting me in quarantine for a day."

We sat in chairs across a small table. I fell all over myself, describing my adventure in the corridor several decks below us. As I was deep into describing the processing room and its operation, she interrupted.

"I know," she said.

"You know what?" I asked.

"Mr. Van Thiem told me about everything—the freighter,

the bodies, burying them in the ocean, the unclaimed body business."

Wait a minute. He told her? "I'm confused," I said.

She had snuck back to the weather room after our little talk in my bathroom, and found Van Thiem waiting for her. A different weatherman was already in her chair, his schedule changed, and three quarantine people were standing nearby, ready to take her pulse, temperature, and blood sample, and walk her to her cabin. Someone had heard her sneeze—maybe someone in another stall as she was hiding her wristband in the bathroom.

The quarantine people had not locked her in, but she was told not to leave her room for a day. They'd be back later to check on her.

Van Thiem visited later in the morning and explained the body dumping operations, including the role of the clandestine freighter, and then asked that she not share the information. It was a patriotic responsibility that helped the nation, and a privilege for the corporation to do it, but Mr. Evans wanted to be low-key about it. It did not, however, excuse her from sneaking past the security fences, nor co-opting me into some kind of secret action. She was politely asked to focus on her job and assume that other activities were well-managed and did not require her participation.

"He was very nice about it, all things considered," she said. "At least, I've still got a job."

So that was it. It was all above board. My paranoia had been wasted. Parker had been truthful, the ship's employees knew about it if they needed to, and the subject was treated respectfully. There was nothing to worry about—Parker, indeed, was just as he had seemed.

Case closed.

If Molly had only asked her bosses in the first place, all of this intrigue and my violating Parker's rules would never have happened. It was a relief, but I was kind of sorry. I had had the pulse of a secret international conspiracy running through my blood, and it felt exciting, even if I had gotten scared and let the demons take over.

I filled her in on my attempts to find her after my encounter with Parker, plus the search the next day in which no one seemed to know her. Was there something sinister going on or not? Why had she been invisible to the crew?

She didn't think anything was wrong, and wasn't much bothered by it. She had been confined to her cabin because of a possible cold or illness. She was never accused of a crime, just bad behavior. She apologized. As to her invisibility with the crew, she wasn't surprised. She was reclusive by nature and didn't socialize, so maybe they really hadn't noticed her in the short time she'd been on the ship.

We both relaxed and visited, then she frowned as a thought came to her. She signaled me to keep talking and took a tablet of paper from a desk drawer. She doodled for a minute, then wrote down a question while I was telling her about my articles. She obviously still didn't trust Big Brother to not be listening in on our conversations.

How many bodies do you think they bring in on a freighter trip?

I hadn't actually counted individual bodies, but if each container had thirty, there'd be around nine hundred bodies in the storage room from the thirty or so containers I saw unloaded. I figured the three crewmen working in the two rooms could handle at least ten or more containers a shift. So that would make about nine hundred bodies over the three or four days between freighter trips, which matched the number being stored.

I wrote down the math while Molly was telling me about the forecast for the coming week. I talked about how I was hoping for a lot of sun so I could work on my tan while Molly was thinking.

She finally wrote:

If the freighter comes every three or four days, and we assume it does that year around, then it does maybe 100 trips a year. That's an average of 90,000 bodies.

Whoa—that was one whopping big number. Something had to be wrong with our figures. Maybe the freighter only came in the summer. But that wouldn't make sense—unclaimed bodies piled up all year long.

Molly kept writing: *How many did Parker say he did?*

He had said ten thousand, and I wrote it down. Her eyes opened wide. It didn't take Parker's brain power to realize he had way understated the number of bodies. Was he misremembering? Had he intentionally lied?

I shrugged. Even if I could have talked about it, I wouldn't have known what to say.

Molly kept writing: *He's doing a lot more bodies than he's telling. Now what?*

I had no idea. While she leaned back and talked about the weather data they received every day from Hawaii, I sat dumbfounded. It's easy to fixate on numbers, but maybe we were wrong about the freighter trips, or the number of containers on each, or even the number of corpses in each container. Maybe the night's delivery was a big one for the month. Maybe, maybe, maybe.

There were so many ways we could be wrong.

But if Parker was intentionally misstating the official body count, then he was either disguising the truth or some of those bags had bodies he wasn't counting. I had seen the body bags and counted the containers, so even if we'd made really bad guesses, I couldn't see myself missing by eighty thousand. Something was wrong. If Parker was quoting only ten thousand, where did the other bodies come from?

We scribbled back and forth for a few more minutes while she took the talking stage to tell me about growing up in

Montana, while I did the thinking. What I wouldn't have given to toss our wristbands off the balcony into the ocean. Not being able to talk freely hobbles my whole system of communication.

I was supposed to be thinking—focusing on the numbers and my list from the night before and all the potential reasons I was being stupid—but instead I found myself listening to Molly as she filled up the time. I'm a reporter, right? Listening is my business, and I couldn't help focusing on her words.

She told me about the family's ranch, surrounded by miles of mountains, forests, and streams, where they all went camping, the horse-packing trips she'd taken, the fishing she'd done. She had fallen in love with weather because there was so much of it in the Big Sky Country, so different and always changing—and having four distinct seasons. She loved Fall best. She talked about the cattle business, the horses she'd grown up with, her brothers, college, and one subject after another to cover up the only subject that really mattered between us.

A part of me wished things were different, because she sounded like a fascinating woman, even as young as she was. A strong woman. The kind that goes on adventures with her eyes wide open. I also couldn't help but notice that she had nothing on under her pajama top. She was well-figured—a whole lot of jiggling as she moved—and the nipples were stiff.

I gave up trying to concentrate on numbers.

Molly's life seemed full, adventurous, and well-lived. It occurred to me that she had never asked to be protected. When she'd come to my cabin, she hadn't talked in terms of being afraid for herself, only the general fear of the unknown, and she certainly hadn't cowered in any corner, expecting that the big, important newspaper reporter should shield her from danger. She was strong, and I liked that. I was accustomed to my daughters and daughters-in-law—

lives always filled with drama and social and personal crises, especially at holidays and vacation times. Even my sons sometimes acted as if they had scripted roles in *As the World Turns.*

She obviously enjoyed talking about her home and family, and it all sounded impressive. I'd grown up in a small town in Texas and had considered my life there to be ordinary and unremarkable. The more she talked, though, the more I thought I needed to improve my resume.

"Have you ever been scuba diving?" I asked innocently. "When I was younger, I used to dive on vacations to Hawaii and the Caribbean. The coral was pretty cool, and I even saw some shipwrecks."

She said something about wishing she could hang out around beaches more, so I knew I had made an impression, even if it was minor. But she followed up with descriptions of a year of college spent in England, and the summer she and a friend had bicycled Europe.

Okay, must be time to wrap up. Besides, I needed to leave before my watching her chest became embarrassing. I fervently hoped she hadn't noticed.

Since Molly had not been locked in and there'd been no betrayal of trust in any conversation Big Brother may have heard, Parker and Van Thiem should be satisfied that we were no threat. Molly expected to be cleared to work her regular shift starting at ten that night, so I suggested we meet for a late lunch the next day at 2. That would give us time to digest what we'd come up with and to consider if there was anything to do. I was no longer concerned about escaping in the helicopter.

We stood and gave each other a hug, which I very much enjoyed. Her embrace was strong. It was a shame about the decades between us. I stopped at the snack bar for a can of beer. I was tired and humbled and puzzled, and needed some-

thing to stop my brain from doing laps. I had missed breakfast, and it was too early for lunch, so I bought a small pizza.

When the beer helped, I went back and got a six-pack.
Hell, I had the rest of the day to recover. After the fourth beer,
I stopped pacing and returned to my conversation with my
computer.

- There's something going on. *Yes.*
- If it's going on here, it may be going on at the other
  facilities. *Yes.*
- There're too many bodies. *Yes.*
- And if it's happening at other facilities, there's way
  too many bodies. *YES!*
- Where would they come from?

I sat back in the chair and thought about that one. I had
Parker's list of cities. Suppose the list didn't include any minor
cities he served? That might account for the extra bodies. I
didn't know how many unclaimed bodies Lubbock, Texas,
had over a year's time, for example, but I was betting a dozen
or less. Okay, so that might be a source, but not for many.

What about transportation? There had to be a substantial
number of trucks involved, and Parker sure as hell wasn't
using FedEx.

To be picking up bodies on a regular basis from any
number of cities across the country, this trucking company
would have to be a pretty significant operation. Surely, somewhere along the line, there'd be an accident and containers
would spill out. Or someone would break into a warehouse
and find a lot more than they were looking for. Or there
would be retired truckers who would talk about their business, and on and on. I read a lot of news sources every day,
and the other reporters and editors read even more. If some-

thing like that had happened, I guarantee you we would have heard about it.

Maybe Parker was also disposing of bodies from Mexico and had just forgotten to add in the number. That would be a lot of bodies.

But why take them to San Francisco? Getting across the border with hundreds of dead bodies would be tough and certainly couldn't be done without somebody noticing. Of course, we can't even stop the live bodies from coming over—maybe dead ones were easier.

Wait a minute. I had forgotten he had trash-cleaning platforms floating in the North Atlantic, too. Wouldn't he use an Atlantic platform to process the bodies from the eastern half of the US? He'd done it for the Ebola crisis. There's not a lot of machinery involved, so building dumping systems on his platforms would be easy. Parker may have infinite money, but not being efficient was against his moral fiber.

Our platform in the Pacific should only be doing the western half of the US, and Parker should be disposing of even fewer bodies. What had he said? There were a hundred thousand total unclaimed bodies per year in the country? Half would be fifty thousand. That made his number of ten thousand still wrong by a factor of five. What was going on? If nothing else, I was now convinced that Parker had been lying through his teeth.

I was suddenly swamped with mysterious bodies.

- Is he hiding something? *Probably*
- If he's hiding something, it must be really worth hiding. *Yes*
- Illegal, immoral, pathological, un-American, unconstitutional? *Maybe*
- World view?

World view? That rang a bell. What was the last thing he'd said to me when we were talking in the processing room?

"Jack, your problem is that you don't have a world view of things. There are real problems on this earth: real, genuine, global problems that require global solutions. It's our duty as citizens of the world to address them, and we shouldn't be squeamish about it. I think I've done something with the ocean cleaning business, and now I'm helping the world in other ways. Treating unwanted bodies is just another version of taking out the trash."

I leaned back in my chair. Global problems? What if Parker was using body bags to address a genuine global problem? What would be another version of trash? What world problems could be solved on the small but highly repetitive scale of dumping bags of something in the ocean?

- Global warming? Would he be putting dry ice in the bags and sinking them to cool the oceans? *Nah.*
- What about global communications? *Nah.*
- What about global literacy? *Nah.*
- What about global conflicts? He could be sinking guns, I guess. Or maybe weaponized poisons, like sarin gas. *Maybe.*
- What about global agriculture? *Nah.*
- What about global terrorism? *Nah.*
- What about dead refugees who had fled to other countries? Hmmmm...
- What about plagues, diseases, pestilence? *Sinking weaponized germs?*
- Global hunger? *Nah.*
- What about overpopulation?

I stopped again, wondering. Controlling overpopulation typically means you either sterilize people or limit the number of total babies, both very long-term solutions. Or you could take the direct route and eliminate people.

The first two possibilities didn't lend themselves to dumping anything in the ocean, but what about killing people? It was a macabre thought, but it could produce a lot of bodies. How you killed them would be a complication, but if you subcontracted that part and considered your part to only be the disposal of bodies, then Parker's offshore side business fits right into the model, as well as into his stress on simply rendering a service. Would Parker, in the darkest corners of his heart, send people to their deaths in order to decrease the population?

I couldn't honestly accept it. But I also couldn't forget what I'd seen him do to his hamster. If he ever convinced himself of the righteousness of a personal crusade—no matter how out-of-bounds someone else might see it—there's no telling what he would do.

That's when it occurred to me that what he'd talked about was treating *unwanted* bodies. He hadn't said *dead* bodies. On the other hand, really not wanting rich, brilliant, two-time-Nobel-Prize-winner Parker Evans to be in the people-killing business, I considered that maybe he was helping solve animal overpopulation.

I had read somewhere that for every child born in America, seventeen puppies or kittens were born. I believe in neutering, for sure, but with numbers like that, society will never catch up.

Were there bunches of dogs and cats in some of those bags? It would be better than killing people, but I certainly understood why it had to be secret. In spite of kill shelters doing it routinely, most of America would go off like a pop-bottle rocket if they found out that killing animals was being done in huge numbers, arbitrarily and secretly.

Maybe it could be those big rats taking over Louisiana, or

even the monster feral hogs overrunning farms and ranches in Texas. But filling up body bags with any kind of regularity would be difficult, and there'd be no reason for it to be a secret.

Nah—it wasn't going to be animals. You don't have a covert international operation to get rid of animals.

I was completely baffled, but what I had to do became perfectly clear.

I had to look inside those bags.

CHAPTER 13

SARAH F's family lost their house. She, her husband, their twelve-year-old son and sixteen-year-old daughter live in a subsidized two-bedroom apartment on the West Side. They've lived in three different apartments over the last nine years.

"We got caught in the 2008 housing collapse," she said. "Jim worked in construction as a senior lead for MiraMax Builders in a new subdivision west of town. We bought one of their new houses in 2002. There was a five-year balloon payment, but it didn't worry us. It seemed like a good investment at the time, and everybody said the value of the house would go up every year. We took that as fact, so we figured we'd refinance after four years and use the equity instead of a cash payment. The company even hired me to do staging for the show homes."

"So, in 2007, you needed to refinance?"

"Yes, but the mortgage mess had begun, and suddenly, what we owed on our house was more than the appraisal, so we had no equity to use for refinancing. We were forced to default, and whoever held our loan at the time booted us right out.

"Jim lost his job because the builder stopped building new houses, and when the company closed, I lost my job too. We were stuck, and we ate up the little savings we had to live on while we looked for work. Our house, by the way, sat empty for three more years. It really burns me when I think we could have been living in it those three years, getting value out of the payments instead of just throwing away our money on rent.

"At least in our latest place, we qualified for the subsidized apartments. I talked the manager into hiring me part-time in the office to do the books, and Jim went to work driving a school bus."

"Did you get food stamps or other kinds of support?"

"We did get food stamps because we'd both lost our jobs at the same time, and there was some IRS deduction we qualified for the first year, but nothing lasted very long or made much difference. Because our incomes are so low, we can't even think about qualifying for another house loan. Jim keeps applying with builders around town, but the market is flooded with younger men who'll work harder, longer, and cheaper. And they give preference to veterans, which is fine but it makes it even tougher to get hired."

"How are the kids doing?"

"Well," Sarah said, pursing her lips and looking away, "not so well. Raymond's done okay but being in middle school now means he's going on a bus instead of walking, and he's home alone on the days I work. He sits and plays video games or stays on his phone, which I don't think is healthy but what can I do? I think he'll be fine.

"It's Cindy I'm worried about. She says riding the bus home because I can't pick her up makes her feel really juvenile. And she wants a new phone, and an iPad, and her own TV, and better clothes. Her dad driving a school bus takes her down a notch in the eyes of the other girls. She's smart as a whip, but the girls are all clique-ish in high school, you know, and they can be really mean to each other. She refuses to invite anybody over, which I understand because our apartment is so small, but she hurts over it and ends up spending a lot of time at other girls' houses.

"Then there's college. All her friends are making big plans, and they want to include her, but we couldn't afford anything close to the university, even with scholarships. She'll have to live at home and go to junior college, and even then she'll need to work for the tuition. I'm sorry, but that's the way it is. Last year, we moved Raymond onto a Murphy bed in the living room, which really sucks, so she could have her own room, but that just gives her a place to close the door and never have to talk to the rest of us. She's got an attitude problem."

"How about your extended family?"

"Well, nobody's rich. My brother lives in Houston, where the housing crunch never really hit, so he's doing good. Jim talked to him once about taking Cindy for her last two years of high school. He's got a sixteen-year-old daughter, too, which would be good for everybody, but I just couldn't live with that. I think she'd see it as an escape plan and would never come home again. I'm her mother, and a girl needs her mother. Besides, you need to learn to suck it up and live with what life gives you."

"What do you see in the future?"

"It all depends on Jim. If he can get back into construction, we'll be better than okay. If not, then we're stuck."

"Any savings? You're a long way from retirement. Do you think you or Jim will ever retire?"

Sarah laughed. "Are you kidding? Everything we had, somebody took from us. All the equity, the 401(k), the second car. I'll be working until I drop dead. And God help us if one of us gets sick."

Jim and Sarah are in their mid-forties. They won't qualify for Social Security for another twenty years, but it won't be much because they're not paying much into it. Even if they both found jobs that let them put aside some amount of money for retirement, it will be at the same time that their expenses go up because their children will be post-high school. Regardless of whatever can be saved towards the future, they'll never make up for the years that they couldn't.

THE FUTURE LOOKS BLEAK. Eight to ten thousand Americans turn sixty-five every day, according to Justice in Aging, a nonprofit that deals with senior citizen poverty. Older Americans were the only demographic for whom poverty rates increased from 2015 to 2016.

That means that as people reach their mid-sixties, they are going to have to either dramatically curtail their spending or keep working to survive. Many are going to go from being near poor to poor.

If today's seniors are struggling with making ends meet based on their current retirement incomes, what will happen to the people of working age today who hold unsteady jobs and have patchwork incomes that leave little to save? The amount of money they contribute to Social Security will be correspondingly less, meaning they will receive less money at withdrawal age. If they have little or no income from other sources like 401(k)s or retirement plans, the situation will be worse, and the first thing to go may be their housing.

CHAPTER 14

"I HAVE to look inside the body bags."

Not able to wait until we sat down, I had written it on a small piece of paper, casually opening it flat on my tray so Molly could read it as we walked around the food stations in the cafeteria.

She glanced at it, her eyes got wide, but she turned away quickly, hoping no one had noticed.

I had lived with my list of questions all morning, arguing back and forth that I might be misinterpreting Parker's mini-lecture on having a *world view* and accepting responsibility to fix global problems. How he had said it seemed so like him—his logical analysis, his no-nonsense approach to problem-solving, and his brutal devotion to a solution once he believed he'd found one. He had attacked the cleaning of the oceans and been successful. Was he now lusting to solve another planet-level problem? In his mind, he's the richest and smartest man in the world, and I have no doubt he believes he's been sanctioned by God to do great things.

But killing people to solve overpopulation? He wouldn't do that.

I grew up with the guy, we had the same Bible Belt values,

we came from the same stock of people, and the same center of the universe. I could not imagine, even with his high-powered brain, that he'd ever believe in a solution that involved taking people's lives.

There must be something else going on.

"We need to talk," she mouthed.

Yes, we do, I thought, but how do we do it this time? I wondered if there wasn't a pulse monitor inside the wrist-band, or some alarm bell that would go off if I removed it. We could do the bathroom trick again, but I wouldn't be surprised if Van Thiem hadn't snuck into my room and installed a listening device in the toilet. Besides, if either Molly or I was to go to the other's room, it would definitely send up a flag to Big Brother.

Wait a minute. "Hot tub," I mouthed back.

She didn't understand. But if we held our wristbands under the water when the tub was bubbling, they wouldn't be able to pick up our voices. I was at least willing to risk it.

Forty-five minutes later, after we'd finished eating and changed, we slid side-by-side into a hot tub on the upper deck. It was a little after mid-afternoon, and we had the place to ourselves. Which was good for me because I didn't want any company. Molly's two-piece bathing suit confirmed the thoughts her pajama top had left to the imagination.

"What do you expect to find?" she said, in a voice louder than the bubbling water. Even if they couldn't hear us, we knew some camera was watching our every move. That meant we had to smile, lean back and enjoy the water, laugh as we swished it around, and look like we had just discovered each other.

"I have no idea," I said, my face turned toward her, smiling, running my fingers softly down her cheek, Molly smiling as if it was exactly what she wanted. "But I have to look. If he's dumping a lot more bodies than he's saying, then there's something else in those bags. Listen to what I've been thinking."

I briefly explained my morning struggles, listed my global problems, and built a case that Parker had to be doing something that would look reasonable and effective to him but would be reprehensible to anybody else. It would be something that would make everyone else at least squeamish and maybe a lot more. The only answer was to look in those bags and find out.

"You're paranoid," she said, her lips close to my ear. "What if you're wrong? What if you don't find anything?"

"If I don't find anything, I'm no worse off. I go back home, and we forget the whole thing. If I don't find anything but get caught doing it, I'll be unceremoniously booted back to Hawaii, which is not far from the position I'm in now. There shouldn't be much risk. All the bags have zippers, which makes it easy to look inside. I sneak into the storage room, open a container, grab a bag, unzip it, take a look, zip it back up, and I'm out of there. My phone's charged up, so I'll take pictures.

"Once I'm back in my cabin, no one will have a clue I ever took a peek. I'm leaving on the helicopter tomorrow morning. If I find something terrible, I'll get to Hawaii and send the Coast Guard back to get you. I want you out of here. You have to trust me."

I laughed as if I had told a joke, and couldn't help using the opportunity to put my arm around her waist under the water. She didn't seem to mind.

"That's why you need to show up tonight for work. You have to be busy while I'm downstairs, so it looks like you had nothing to do with it."

"Why don't you contact somebody? Tell them what you think is happening? They could get on that freighter and look. Send an email to your wife or your editor."

I smiled, leaned my head back against the tub's rim, took a deep breath, then turned to her again. "The internet's been down for a couple of days. There was an alert saying the satellite connection was on the blink, so phones don't work either. I wonder if it's related to us."

"Now you really are paranoid," she said as she rolled over, swung her leg across to straddle me, and leaned her face next to my ear.

The only natural place for my hands was on her thighs, close to her ass.

"All this business—it just can't be true. I bet our numbers were just way off or something. I do weather, remember? I'm not good at understanding the past that I know, much less understanding the future that I don't. You need to make sure you're not talking yourself into fantasy land."

Molly kissed my ear, then swung her leg over in a dismount and resumed her position beside me. We talked for a few more minutes, then separated, eyes closed, just thinking. Paranoia is not something I admire, but sometimes, you have to have a little to find the truth.

That's not all. Oh my God, I needed a drink! It had been a long, long time since I'd been cheek-to-cheek with a mature woman who wasn't my wife, and even then, contact like this with Beth was so far in the past that I couldn't remember. And that's not to mention how smooth Molly's legs felt and the press of those glorious nipples against my chest. When she leaned in next to my face, it was all I could do not to kiss her. Thank God she had slid off before I was hard enough to embarrass myself. I hoped we wouldn't be standing up anytime soon.

Idiot! What was I—a kid back in junior high? I hoped God wasn't watching. Some of my friends had granddaughters her age. And even if age should have stopped me, I shouldn't feel this way to begin with. Had my brain been rocked by the waves too much, or what?

I forced myself to think about Parker.

If I was caught before I got to the bags, then I would confess to absolute stupidity and tell Parker the truth—that I didn't believe anything he'd said about the bodies. Parker would give me a tongue-lashing, slap my wrists, complain to the owner of the paper, and get a bank of lawyers involved so I could never write anything about his operations. My editor would be pissed, the owner would be pissed, and I might even get fired. That's not a sound path to retirement.

If I was caught after I got to the bags and had found nothing inside to disprove what he said, I would again confess to absolute stupidity, with the same results.

Let's be reasonable—if he has nothing to hide, then I'm not going to find it.

But if he is hiding something inside those body bags, I needed to find out what it is. If it's something bad enough to be a crime? So bad he could never have it revealed? Bad enough that I would never be allowed to tell anyone about it? What then? What about being safe?

I refused to think about it. Safe be damned. I had to look inside those bags, and I'd just have to make sure I wasn't caught.

———

I CHOSE two o'clock in the morning. If the body-dumping boys were at work—I assumed they would be—I could sneak into the storage room when the forklift operator was in the mechanical room. If I timed it right, I'd have several minutes to open a container, look in a few bags, take pictures, close the container, and sneak out.

If the body processing plant wasn't operating and all the rooms were locked, I'd try opening the storage room with my knife. If that didn't work, I'd give up and go back to my room— no harm, no foul. But it wouldn't make my suspicions go away.

Could I do anything after I was back home? Well, maybe. I might be able to find the home port of the freighter, or find some of the routes of the trucks. Given that, I might be able to intercept containers and inspect them in the middle of their transit.

The major problem with working things from that end was that even if I did find something wrong, it would be far removed from Parker Evans. He'd never be connected to anything that wasn't found in his back pocket. Considering how many lawyers he must have, I wasn't sure there was any way to make a criminal charge stick except with a photo of him holding a knife, standing next to an unzipped body bag that had a cut-up body hanging out of it. Maybe he'd even have to autograph it.

The only way this was going to work was if I got a look in the bags just before they were shoved into the deep-sea sausage.

My phone dinged at 2 a.m.

The first maneuver was to leave my wristband on the bed, then head over the balcony railing to avoid any cameras, and climb down two levels to the passenger deck. Luckily, my balcony was close enough to the deck that I could climb up when I got back. I may be older than dirt, but I figured my height would let me grab a couple of railings and monkey up to my room. There were no outside lights on that deck, so I didn't worry about being seen.

It worked without too much embarrassment, and I nervously walked to the stern, staying in the shadows as I went over the gates, carefully passing through the service door and stepping back down to the double doors. My knife again wiggled the latch open, and I slipped into the dark corridor. It was as I'd hoped—the two sets of tall doors at the far end were open, spilling light into the corridor, and I could hear the conveyor belt. I gave myself a mental pat on the back and started forward.

I kept to the side as I slipped down the corridor and again tucked myself behind the bulkhead. I waited for the forklift to retrieve a container and take it across the hall, then slipped through the open door and scrambled to the back of the room.

I crammed myself behind one of the containers, enough to be hidden. I was in no rush. I was ready to open as many containers and bags as needed to either confirm or deny any of my theories. It might take several minutes of dodging the forklift operator, but I was determined to be patient and methodical.

The forklift came back with an empty container, stacked it close to the front wall, turned, and took another container out of the room. Assuming he would continue in that order, I set my sights on the container to my left that was farthest from the door, stood up, and yanked on the lid.

It was locked.

Damn! Damn! Damn!

I struggled to push, pry, and jerk, all to no avail. I huffed, listened to the noises outside, then started looking for keys. The lock was the type found on home freezers: a small open cylinder with multiple rectangular teeth on the end, so one key should open any container. If I was the forklift operator, I'd have a hook on the wall someplace with an extra key or two, just in case. If I couldn't find a real key, I'd try to jimmy it with my knife, but that might either ruin the lock without opening it or break the blade.

I reminded myself that I could always scuttle back out the door, go to my cabin, and be no worse off. If I was discovered along the way, I was at least guaranteed that my plea of stupidity would work because all I had to do was be honest. Parker would be too busy laughing at me to think of getting even.

But my luck held—there were extra container keys hanging next to the door, and I had just taken one off the wall when I heard the forklift coming back. I ducked behind the closest container and squeezed against the wall to make myself as small as possible while he did his cargo exchange.

As he motored back through the door, I went back to the container—and the key worked. With a crack of only an inch, a chill whipped over my fingers.

The container was a freezer.

Well, duh. It made sense. If the bodies weren't frozen, at the very least, they'd stink to high heaven since the zipper could never keep the smell of rotting bodies from leaking. Someone, somewhere would be sure to investigate what was in those bags.

I raised the lid fully up. I could see the edges of three, maybe four body bags, all lumpy and twisted from sliding back and forth in the container. Some had the zippers facing up, others down, and some bags were squished or collapsed at the side or the ends. I grabbed the edges of the topmost bag and pulled it to expose the upper half of the zipper, surprised by how frigid the plastic was. There had to be some sort of battery-powered refrigeration unit incorporated into the container, or maybe some way of adding dry ice to keep the insides so cold.

Grabbing the zipper burned my thumb and finger. I gave them a quick breath, then grabbed again, harder, and struggled to get the zipper half open. A man's face looked back at me. Frost highlighted his eyelashes and brows and hair, and clung to wrinkles in his skin. A pattern of sutures across his chest made it look like one of those post-autopsy corpses on the TV cop shows, exactly like a coroner would do. Pulling my phone from my pocket, I took three pictures from different angles.

I pulled the zipper back up, wrestled the bag below it up to the top, and opened it. This body did not resemble the first. It was an older man with a dirty, unshaven face, his hair long, stringy and all matted to one side, with layers of frost covering a stiff, dirty t-shirt. He was completely clothed.

Looking closely at the face, the neck, and the hands, inspecting the clothes, I knew exactly what I was seeing. In my weeks of interviewing the homeless, I had met people like this every day. As much as others may dress differently, many of the street people took on a common patina: thrift store shirts and pants worn threadbare, torn, full of wrinkles. The cuffs and collars were uniformly ragged, the pants sometimes belted, sometimes roped, sometimes aided by suspenders, and a mishmash of jackets, coats, sweaters, or hoodie sweatshirts covered with stains and spills.

I took four pictures, zipped the bag back up, and shoved it aside as I wrestled up another one, my hands freezing again from touching the plastic. Getting the third bag was harder, with the first two on top of it. I finally got most of the zipper exposed and was ready to open it when I heard the whine of the forklift—it was coming!

I closed the container lid quickly and had barely enough time to squirrel myself to the side of the container when the forklift rolled in. The driver quickly added an empty container to a separate stack away from the others, then lifted a new one and went out. I returned to my inspection of the container.

The third body was clothed like the second—a Black woman wearing shabby pants and shirt, a jacket torn around the shoulders, dirty fingernails, face and hands. Her throat had been cut, soaking her clothes with blood, leaving no doubt about the cause of death. I took pictures, zipped it up, and tried for a fourth bag. It was too buried to pull up, so I closed the container and moved on to the next one. I wanted to see more bags, both out of curiosity and from the horror I was barely able to comprehend. How could these bodies be so intermingled? Did no one—no one at all—know the difference between the bodies Parker collected as part of his regular business and those that surely had been brutally murdered?

I kept my head down, intent on seeing more.

The next container yielded two bodies with sutures, one of them with clothes on. After hurriedly photographing them, I closed the lid and opened another container, unzipping the top bag. Inside was a frozen woman with a yellow bandanna around her head.

I screamed, stifled it, and fell back, not wanting to believe it was her. How long had it been since I had looked for Sally— weeks, even months? Had she been dead that long, or had she been hanging out someplace before someone turned her into a corpse?

What was I feeling? Remorse? Surprise? Resignation? How about anger? I had considered Crazy Sally someone who was circling the drain, but that didn't give anyone the right to kill her as if she didn't matter.

I felt my heart beating, and my breath coming in short spurts.

Memories flooded my brain, remembering what I had seen and said and felt as I'd blithely conducted my interview. I remembered my own callousness as I grouped her into the unable-to-be-helped category.

I slowly forced myself to turn back to the body and look more closely. The face was too thin, too worn, too old. It wasn't Sally at all. It wasn't even the same pattern on the bandanna.

I took a deep breath, but I couldn't shake the fright from my mind.

The immediate scare of thinking it was Sally, that it was someone I had talked to and written about, someone I'd spent time with, had me rattled. It's one thing to realize someone had been deliberately murdering homeless people, but thinking it had happened to someone I knew shocked me to the core and made this horror feel personal. Even when I knew it wasn't her, that pain in my gut, that intimate shock, still welled up inside me, and I fumed with anger.

Yes, it wasn't Sally, but I was sure it could have been her, that it could have been any of the poor, wretched, homeless people I'd met. That made this crime, this hideous, intentional, hateful crime, even more wrong. It had to be exposed, it had to be stopped, and whoever was doing it had to be punished!

I held myself in check enough to get pictures of the woman, her wound, the inside of the container, and then more of the storage room and the stacks of containers around me.

Okay. My heart and mind were burning. I'd seen enough. I lowered the lid, locked it, slipped the key into my pocket, timed my exit to follow the forklift out the door, and faded into the darkness of the corridor. It took less than ten minutes to get to the passenger deck below my balcony and face the monkey climb up to my balcony.

Misjudging my wall-scaling talents, it took more effort than I'd expected, but I finally rolled myself over the balcony rail, dumped myself onto the deck, then took a moment to quiet my heaving chest. Not bothering to get up, I reached for the handle of the sliding glass door, clumsily pulled it open, crawled through, and slid it shut with my foot.

Seeing no Van Thiem set to pounce on me, I struggled to regain my composure, taking slow, deep breaths and thinking in sequence about what I had seen. Those thousands of extra bodies were no accident. Someone was using Parker's service to get rid of the bodies of murdered homeless people. If I could find them in random containers on a randomly timed visit, then these extra bodies in the containers had to be a regular feature, which meant there had to be a lot of them.

Parker had told me he was running a legitimate business, a nationwide service to help the economy and the environment. He had quotable numbers of bodies, he had a printed list of the locations of sources I had held in my hand, and I'd even seen barcodes on the bags—it all looked real, it all looked authentic, it even looked well-managed. Could he have been deceived and someone else was slipping the bodies into the process? Was somebody using Parker's services to hide the murdering of a substantial slice of the population? Did Parker's numbers simply come from a spreadsheet or business manifest so he really didn't know what was going on?

Maybe Parker's business was only picking up body bags, and he had no knowledge of where the bodies came from or how many were outside of his intentions. I argued that it had to be true, that he was innocent and knew nothing. But I kept admitting to myself that it wasn't likely. It was Parker's nature to know everything about what he controlled. If he did know about the extra bodies, I was left with a frightening question: Had he also been responsible for their deaths?

Did he see the killing of the homeless as just another way of taking out the trash?

CHAPTER 15

I HAD BEEN TOLD the helicopter would be leaving Hawaii at six and picking me up nine-thirty in the morning. It was my sole lifeline, and I desperately wanted to get off this ship.

Molly had returned to her ten-to-six shift in the weather room. That guaranteed she'd be fully accounted for while I was sneaking around downstairs. Now that I'd returned from my exploration, I was itching to fill her in with the details. It wasn't much past three in the dark of the night, so I knew she'd still be in the weather room. But if I went there, I knew the cameras, my wristband, or both would make clear what I was doing when I should have been fast asleep. As much as I wanted to talk to her immediately, I had to be satisfied with sticking to our planned six o'clock rendezvous.

I was in the cafeteria at 5:30, trying not to look like my stomach was churning.

I was still there, alone, an hour later.

At 6:30, I gave up and hurried to her cabin in case she had gone there for some reason. I knocked several times, but there was no reply. Thinking maybe she'd been caught up in something in the weather room, I ran upstairs and quietly walked past the door. Only the one chair was occupied, and not by

Molly. I didn't know what to think. I walked the hallways, the atrium, the cafeteria twice, and kept going back to her cabin.

Nothing. No hint of where she was or what had happened. I was concerned about being ready for the helicopter, so I finally abandoned the search and went back to my room.

At 8:30, I was waiting on the steps to the landing pad with my bag. I would get to Hawaii, get to the Coast Guard, and show them my pictures. I didn't have any proof that something illegal was happening, but the pictures of the wounds on the bodies should at least get them interested enough to visit Parker's ship. If I could convince them Molly was in danger, they might move faster.

At 10:30, with a growing sense of dread, I admitted to myself that I wasn't going anywhere. I sat on the steps trying to breathe, my insides tight, my stomach aching, and my forehead dripping with sweat. How had I been found out? Had they expected it and followed my every move? Was I seen by the forklift operator? Was there a camera in the storage room?

Or was there actually no helicopter coming? Had they always planned on never letting me leave?

I had wanted to believe that Parker was not part of the killing scheme, that someone else was adding the bodies of murdered people into his legitimate unclaimed body disposal process and that he didn't know. But now Molly was missing, and my helicopter hadn't appeared. Maybe Parker *was* involved. Even if it was only providing the service for a warlord or a terrorist or some right-wing or left-wing group with a vendetta against the homeless, it made him an accomplice, a connection he could never allow to be exposed.

It would be worse if he was the instigator. All my mental gyrations of the night before had connected him to population control or people management for the good of the country or as simple as economic improvement, and those connections suddenly didn't seem so remote or impossible.

Once again, if Parker had felt that he'd been ordained by God to improve the world, I could see him defying his upbringing to make it happen.

I did not—*did not*—want to believe it. Maybe Molly was on the barge monitoring the ocean's temperature, maybe my helicopter was only late, maybe, maybe. Maybe all I needed to do was relax and wait.

My body was telling me differently. The sweat on my forehead and hands was from being scared. My heart was beating from desperation, and my stomach was churning from the suspicion I was being played. Parker was letting every muscle in my body knot up with each minute spent waiting and worrying, waiting until my brain exploded from the bone-chilling conviction I had discovered something they could not, would not allow to be known.

Molly may have already been taken care of, and now it was my turn.

What could I do? The only tangible evidence was the photographs. The internet was down, again another unbelievable coincidence, so I couldn't get my pictures to anyone or even tell anyone they existed. Tell the crew what I'd found? Harold Plackery, the communications tech, seemed like a good guy. I couldn't imagine he would have been recruited by Parker as part of the conspiracy to hide the body dumping business, and he could even be the key to getting my pictures out to the rest of the world. But I couldn't be sure he wouldn't just laugh and turn me over to Parker.

Damn it!

Maybe I should scream everything I knew to everyone in the dining room at lunchtime. Just tell everybody! Show everyone the pictures until every one of them knew what I had found. But I couldn't be sure they wouldn't all wrestle me to the ground and turn me over to Parker.

Damn it!

With my bag in hand and dreading every step, I returned to my cabin to find Van Thiem waiting for me. We didn't need to speak. I set my bag on the bed, he frisked me, taking my phone and knife, then shoved me out the door.

It didn't take long to be marched back to the palace. Parker was in the front reception room, staring out the window, watching the wrap-up of the morning dumping of the lagoon. He didn't appear overly concerned, or worried, or angry, or especially thoughtful. He only stood at the window, watching as if there was nothing else to do.

Van Thiem pointed me into an overstuffed chair.

"Where's Molly?" I asked.

Parker seemed not to hear. Instead, he talked to the window in a soft voice. "We've been doing this for more than ten years. When we began, there was almost ninety million metric tons of plastic crap where we are, and we've decreased it by 11 percent. That's not too bad, considering about eight million tons gets added globally every year, but I had hoped, really hoped, for more.

"People told you that the isolation gets to them? Or the wave action? It's not for me. It's seeing trash every day. Every day, from horizon to horizon. We keep sweeping it up, sucking it out, carrying it off, but our efforts seem so small, and the horizon seems so very far away. Every day, I hope tomorrow will look different, will look cleaner and healthier. Every day, I hope to see stretches of water not dotted with all this crap bobbing up and down. It's been ten years, and it's still out there, boiling up with the waves, mocking me as if it's laughing at my feeble attempts to make a difference.

"I shouldn't be too hard on myself," he said as he turned to me. "We deliberately stay where the floating trash is the heaviest because that's where the sludge is the thickest. It's ironic, but the skirt works best with thick sludge. When it's thin, it doesn't resist the electric field as much and leaks through the fabric.

"My lot in life, I guess, is to be patient while I suffer along with the earth."

"Where's Molly?" I said more loudly.

"Your hot tub sweetie? I'm afraid that her cold got much worse, and she's on her way to Hawaii."

"That's not true," I said, barely keeping from yelling it out. "She didn't have a cold to begin with, and there's been no helicopter. I've been watching all morning, and nothing has come."

Parker looked at me with a calm face, then smirked and shrugged. "Well, we let her swim for it."

My jaw dropped, and the light dimmed. I had pushed myself forward in the chair, getting my legs ready to stand, preparing to be defiant and forceful and confrontational, and to yell and scream and tell him that he had been revealed, that I knew what he was doing, that he had been caught, and that he was going to jail for the rest of his life.

Now, I couldn't muster any sound at all. I collapsed into the back of the chair, my legs going out in front of me, the air rushing out of my lungs. I felt myself going flat. I gasped for air and didn't find enough.

Molly was dead. That sweet child, that strong woman. She'd probably been dead for hours, never having had a chance to survive.

I wanted to grab Parker by the neck and choke the life out of him, but I had no strength. I'd collapsed like a deflated balloon, horrified by an image of Molly out in the rolling trash, impossible to see from the ship as she flailed away. Why would she even bother to swim? What good would it have done? She could tread water, her legs going back and forth, her small voice screaming and crying for help, while no sound would have been heard by anyone. Her energy would have drained away, and she would have gone under, her lungs filling with pieces of plastic, mouthfuls of sludge, the air coming up, out of her throat, until there was no air left.

"You know everything, don't you?" I muttered quietly, trying not to sound naive or stupid. "You know all about those thousands of extra bodies in the containers, don't you? You know about them being murdered and your noble *national service* being used to do away with their bodies, don't you?"

"You know, Jack," Parker said as he watched me founder, "the problem is that you don't have a world view."

Everything inside me suddenly burst. I launched myself out of the chair and had almost reached him when Van Thiem kicked my legs out from under me. I crashed to the floor. He rammed his foot into my diaphragm, and I stopped breathing, doubled up in pain, holding my arms tight across my middle, hiding it from another kick.

Van Thiem grabbed me under the chin and half-lifted, half-threw me back into the chair. I was significantly bigger than him, but I couldn't resist, couldn't even think about resisting.

"The world view, Jack," Parker continued as if nothing had happened. "Are you listening? What keeps us from being a great people? Sympathy. Plain old sympathy. We feel sorry for people or animals or our society or ourselves, and it makes us weak. And because we're weak, we shy away from making hard decisions. And when we can't make hard decisions, we make bad decisions.

"Look at this planet, this poor old worn-out planet. We knew the problems plastics would bring from the very first, but we sympathized with our invention, thinking we were deserving, that innovation should take precedence over any damage that might result. Of course, we didn't realize people would be so flagrant about their trash, and that it would pollute our environment so completely.

"Not to worry, though: We looked at our wide-open plains and big rivers and our immense oceans and thought that each was infinite. We never imagined the people of the world would dirty things up so quickly. When we invent something new, we see all the wonderful results it will produce and innocently assume it will always be worth the cost. So much self-reinforcement, so much self-centeredness, Jack, so many bad decisions."

"That makes it okay to kill people?" I finally squeaked out between gasps. "I know what they look like, Parker. I know the clothes they wear, I know the unshaven faces, the bags under their eyes from malnutrition and hunger. I know what they look like because I've sat with them, I've listened to them, I've *cared* about those people!"

Parker leaned down until he could look me in the eyes.

"There you go! Perfect example. I read your newspaper articles, Jack, and liked them. I even shared them with my senior managers. Why do you think I did that? To show the goodness of sympathy and mercy? To illustrate how we should all have compassion for the downtrodden? Nope, sorry. I used those articles to show my managers what losers look like: people who can't make it in this world.

"In any other species, losers are left to die. Think about it —are there any unemployed ducks on duck welfare? Any starving deer being fed by other deer? Any cows wanting compensation for being raised only to become hamburgers? Our street corners are full of people who are sucking the life out of towns and cities, destroying our ability to move forward. You talked to people who were frauds, Jack, and then you made it seem as if they had inherent value, as if they were worth something.

"You were wrong. They...are...worth...nothing.

"They keep standing on the street corners begging for money because people keep giving it to them. People help them out with money and food and tons of sympathy. They're allowed to continue being weak and dependent because of people like you. You argue for their salvation, their rescue, their rejuvenation to become useful citizens, and—the reason I really like—that it's a noble thing to save those who are less fortunate than the rest of us. You drip with compassion and self-righteousness while rejecting any real solutions as being beneath us as a society.

"You refuse to make hard decisions."

He moved to a long side table with a ship model on it and opened a center drawer. Taking out a sheet of paper and a colored marker, he slid the drawer closed and moved to the well-polished oak end table next to my overstuffed chair.

"Let's play a game, shall we? Let's imagine I have a magic button."

Kneeling next to the end table and placing the paper on top, he drew a circle the size of a fifty-cent piece and colored it red with the marker.

"It's a simple button, but I'm going to give it magical powers."

He pointed at the overstuffed chair opposite me. "Suppose there's a man sitting in that chair. Let's make him one of your homeless buddies. He's old, he's sick, he can't stand up straight, he can't even think straight. He pees his pants but refuses to wear adult diapers because he thinks they're beneath his dignity. He smells bad. There is no job he can do, even of the simplest kind. He limps in a crooked shuffle, and gasps for air because his lungs don't work because he smoked for years.

"Now, regardless of the fact that his condition is the result of choices he made in his life, you have to support him. From out of the meager salary of a hack newspaper reporter, you have to provide him with shelter, you have to buy him food, you have to protect him and be kind to him and talk to him, even though you don't want your kids to be around him. In fact, you hope your kids avoid him, because you're afraid he'll become as big a drain on their lives as he is on yours. In reality, in the back of your mind where you try to ignore it, you wish he would die so you can get back to a normal life.

"Now, take your finger, come on, take your finger," he grabbed my hand so that my index finger stood out, "and put it above the button. If you push this magic button, he's gone. No pain, no lingering, no cost, no law-breaking, no condemnation from others, no concerns from friends or relatives, no anything. He just disappears, and you won't even feel guilt. After you press that button, there is no one—absolutely no one—who will hold you responsible.

"Would you do it? If you could walk away with a clean conscience, with no regret, with no remorse, because he just—poof!—disappeared, would you do it?"

He hesitated, then forced my finger onto his magic button.

It wasn't a fair game. I couldn't argue or discuss it or tell him why I wouldn't do it. Damn it, it wasn't something you could arbitrarily mandate for people. You can't make decisions about other people's deaths without morality being involved, or values, or a fundamental belief in something bigger than you, or that it shouldn't be you who's making the decision. Every person has value. Every person has worth.

"You can't throw people away!" I screamed.

"See, didn't I tell you? You can't even admit that pushing the button felt good. You're a natural-born coward. Remember the old Black man from your article? I just described him. He's worthless now, but he'll really be worthless in a couple of years. Why not push the button? Why not relieve him of his misery?"

He put his hands on the table and looked me in the eye. "Why not relieve you of your misery?"

He stood up. "Let's take them out of the economy while

we're at it. The money budgeted for social services for them can be put into schools. More teachers, better salaries, better facilities, more activities. Wouldn't it be worth it, Jack? Wouldn't it be better to use the money for something good, something that will pay off?"

I leaned forward, trying to get over my hurt, vigorously shaking my head from side to side.

"I'm not saying don't be compassionate," Parker went on. "I'm just saying be compassionate where you get a good return. Pick the targets of your compassion, so it'll actually be effective, where it's an investment in what is viable and usable and does good in the world. Get rid of the bad returns because they destroy the good returns. No return, no compassion."

He backed away and began walking back and forth across the room as if he were delivering a lecture.

"Your kind of people get in my way because you have compassion for something that has no value, no worth, and never will. My little button is good for one person, but the world view is that there needs to be a bigger button. Every nation has the dregs of their society that feed off of everyone else, a layer of their population that's full of bottom-feeders who provide nothing to anyone but still demands they be taken care of. They drain their nation just like ours drain our nation."

Now Parker was preaching like he was behind a pulpit.

"It takes people like me to make the hard decisions, to see the truths of the world and to react in a reasonable way to save it. If it weren't for me, our oceans would be choking to death by now, and everyone would be standing around with their thumbs up their asses wondering what happened. If it weren't for me, the country would be spiraling into debt even worse because we'd be feeding millions more of the unworthy, the slackers, the bums, the lazy, the incapable, and the incompetent. I'm the one keeping us on an even keel, Jack. It's because of me that we have any future at all."

I was feeling sick, and my stomach was hurting like crazy. But my hate was growing. Blind, stupid, terrible hate, and Parker was the target of every bit of it.

"Killing people? That's your answer? You're applauding yourself because you think that by killing people, you're saving the country? You're just an arrogant bastard!" I screamed, struggling to stand up and shout back at him. Van Thiem shoved me down again.

Parker continued his rant, his voice ratcheting up. "Arrogant? You call me arrogant? I'm not arrogant, I'm honest. I can make the hard decisions. I'm the one! The rest of you cry and moan and groan and piss along like children waiting for an adult to save you. Well, I'm the adult, and you love it because you don't have to take responsibility anymore."

"Responsibility?" I shot back. "You're talking to me about responsibility? To who? To you? You're nothing but a damned back alley thug who's killing anybody he doesn't like. Don't talk to me as if you've found the solution to human misery!"

Parker's face turned red and he flailed his arms, frustration growing at my refusal to agree with him. I wondered if he was going to open a window and kick my ass over the side of the ship. He walked up and down and finally stopped on the plush carpet in front of me.

"Jack, you're misunderstanding me, again. I don't *kill* anyone," he said in softer tone.

He could settle down all he wanted, but I was going to shout. "I looked in the bags, Parker. I looked in the bags! You're filling bags with homeless people as fast as you can, and you're flushing them down to the bottom of the ocean."

"Well," Parker said, again with that damned smirk, "that last part I'll take credit for. But what you don't understand is that I'm in the bag disposal business, Jack, not the killing business. I just pick up the trash and put it where no one will ever see it again."

He shrugged as if he was totally innocent.

I looked up at him. Had I missed something? What kind of crap was he talking now? "What do you mean?"

Parker actually smiled. "Oh, this is the part I like best. It's all done by software."

My mind was blank with confusion and my face must have shown it.

CHAPTER 16

"IT's a little thing I played with in graduate school," Parker said. "I had to create an error generator to test a program I'd written for a systems control class. Once I activated it, the error generator would try to defeat my control software by sending it bad data.

"To make it a good test, though, I couldn't know when it would attack or from where or how, so I created a program that, once it was started, jumped from one computer to another, sending errors and interruptions to my control program. I had no idea when or how it would attempt to disrupt my controls. It's not such a big thing now, but it was then.

"Well, once I had my ocean cleaning business up and going, I thought I'd help the country out with some of its other problems, like food shortages, weather, drugs, education, immigration overload, overburdening of resources, and all that stuff. To choose something practical to address where I could make an immediate difference, I modified my old program to crawl around the web and gather national statistics, first of the economy, then of natural resources, then population demographics, and whatever. I set the program to mix those numbers together and determine what problem needed attention first.

"The choice was surprisingly clear, and something I hadn't anticipated. Did you know there's a slice of our population that not only doesn't contribute anything to our society but constantly drains its resources? It's destructive in both directions. It's people who produce no knowledge, no progress, no economic value, no societal thinking, nothing, and yet feed off the rest of us—money, food, square footage, other people's emotions, their concerns, their time."

Parker's voice took on the tone of an elitist professor.

"The program worked very well. Then I thought of something else it could do. Since it figured out the biggest drain on our society—which turns out to be all your friends standing on street corners, sleeping in tents, badgering people to give them money—why not let it help get rid of them?

"I enhanced my program to routinely place online job ads aimed at certain well-recognized groups of people—White supremacists, Black supremacists, the KKK, the Nazis and skinheads, Mexican gangs, various unhinged groups of one flavor or another—in general, those groups who have a deep hatred for someone, usually several someones, both on the right and the left.

"Running completely independent of me and on some computer in some network that I'm not associated with, the program advertises that bags are available for the collection of an item with certain characteristics. Whoever is interested in earning a little money—it doesn't matter who or where they are or where the item comes from—can order a bag and then go about collecting the item. When the item is procured, they use the app on their phone to take a picture of the barcode on the bag. Once the bag is procured, the barcode is matched to the barcode on their phone, and the person who put the item in it gets paid."

I sat stunned for a moment. Bag? Barcode? Suddenly, the pieces came together—the barcodes I'd seen going up the conveyor belt. They represented a *bounty guarantee* for any single member of the particular group targeted by the program.

The *bag* Parker referred to was a body bag, and the *item* was the body of a homeless person.

I managed to straighten up in my seat and lean forward. "Let me see if I get this straight: You have a robot program running over the internet offering money for people to kill other people. The person who buys a body bag kills someone, puts the body in a body bag and leaves it somewhere. When it's picked up, the barcode is read, and when it matches the barcode on the phone of the killer, your program pays that person some amount of money."

Parker had a broad smile. "You may be getting smart in your old age, Jack. I don't know who it is that gets put in the body bag, I don't know who it was that put them there, or where, or when. And nobody knows it's me because all they see are messages from some computer app.

"All the money transactions are by bitcoin, so how's that for being progressive? My program sends payment to the phone in bitcoins, and then the owner of the phone redeems the coins at banks that pull real money from a ghost account in the Bahamas."

His smile had elevated itself to a grin of pure delight.

"I call these groups my *network of hate*. Isn't that cool-sounding? It fulfills certain people, you see, to kill someone. It makes them feel good about themselves and gives them a real sense of contributing to society. Think about how it builds their self-esteem, Jack. It's people doing what they want to do. My program just nudges them in a particular direction with a little incentive, and then handles the mechanics of the trans-actions. I'd bet you a dollar that it decreases crime in the inner cities, since my contractors aren't anxious to kill people randomly because they get to do it on a regular basis, and get paid for it, too."

"You think that because you have a program doing it that you're not guilty? You're stupid. I've seen the bodies downstairs. Their blood is on your hands."

Parker's face contorted, and he flew into a rage. Even as a kid, he never liked being contradicted.

"My hands are clean!" he yelled. "Those bodies earned every bit of what they got!"

His hands were shaking, his face was steaming, and he was as close to losing control as I've ever seen anyone. I sat back in my chair and savored the moment, forcing myself to smile, which incensed him even more. It took a couple of minutes for Parker to settle down.

"Let me continue," Parker said in a steady voice, though his eyes were burning through me. "Once the item is acquired, there are independent vendors—again, who only see a message from my program—that pick up the bag at the GPS coordinates of the disposal site. The people picking up the bag don't know what's in it or who put it there, but they take it and deposit it in a freezer in some warehouse. When the freezer fills up, it's scheduled for pickup by truckers who know that the bags inside the freezer contains bodies, but they think the warehouse is owned by the city and used to store overflow from a morgue.

"And since all the services are free, nobody ever questions the operation.

"That is, nobody did until you came along. You had to listen to that silly little girl, and she got you all hot and bothered about some strange ship in the night, so you go sneaking around and find out about our side business. Damn it, Jack, you should have quit there—just left it alone. You should have *believed* me. But no, you had to go back and look in the bags. Now you've started something that is out of my control."

My pain had decreased enough that I was able to follow his words, but I still couldn't believe this wasn't some big joke. Could you really do all this without somebody noticing? Did no one suspect anything? Even the guys downstairs, sliding bodies into the sausage: Was Parker so convinced of his secrecy that he could count on them never unzipping a single bag and thinking that maybe something was strange about a body being fully clothed?

I was exhausted. I sat dumbfounded, shaking my head. This couldn't really be happening. It was murder by proxy, all determined by a damn computer program. I shook my head. How could I have even imagined that Parker couldn't be responsible for everything I had seen?

A sharp pain hit my neck. I jumped, but Van Thiem's hand on my shoulder kept me in the chair. He pulled a needle from my skin as I wobbled, then slid onto the floor.

The last thing I saw was Parker smirking, leaning over, holding his finger above the red circle he had drawn on the paper.

He pressed his button, and everything went black.

CHAPTER 17

I FEEL AWFUL. I mean really awful, like the worst hangover ever after my body had been whipped with chains. That's pretty awful, but I actually feel worse than that. My brain had crawled outside my head. I can't think straight, I'm all squashed up, my legs are up near my chest, and my head is pushed to one side. I'm choking on something, something nasty, some kind of grainy powder. My hands are trying to grab onto something, but they slide off because it's slick.

It's dark, really dark, pitch-black dark. I can't tell if my eyes are open or not, but I can feel them stinging like crazy. It's like I'm all wrapped up or something.

The drug is wearing off, and I'm becoming more aware. Suddenly, my blood pressure shoots through the roof, and my panic overwhelms everything. I'm trying to get my legs to do something, but I'm upside down, so my legs won't stretch out. I struggle to get right side up, and when I finally do, my legs straighten out along with my hands and arms. I'm pulling against jelly, pushing against big lumps of dough and then hard things, and I hear noise all around me. My brain finally processes the noise, and I slowly realize what I'm hearing.

It's a conveyor belt.

Damn. There's no mistaking that sound, and it tells me where I am.

I'm in a body bag. I'm in a body bag, inside the deep-sea sausage in the body processing room, on my way to the bottom of the ocean.

I'm pulling out of my haze, and panic is overwhelming me. I hack and cough and vomit. Disinfectant. It's the disinfectant that's killing my eyes and making me choke. My legs are moving up and down, trying to stay steady on something, but it feels like I'm sliding on ice. My hands are running up and down the bag, and I'm gasping for breath but only getting more disinfectant in my lungs. I cough and vomit more. It takes all my focus, but I slow my breathing down and make myself inhale shallow gulps of air.

My knife. Do I have my knife? I'm jamming my hands into my pockets, then remember Van Thiem taking my knife. I feel my wallet, my handkerchief, dimes, nickels, quarters, nail clippers, and the refrigerator key I forgot to hang back on the peg. My pen is gone, and I'm hearing the conveyor belt grind and wobble, and panic's making my face gush sweat. I'm feeling hot, real hot at the same time everything pressing against me is freezing cold.

I gag and then vomit again. Wiping my lips with the back of my hand, I grab my handkerchief and wipe my eyes, blow my nose, and then hold it over my face.

Bodies are mashed up against me. That was the jelly and the dough and the hard things—bodies and heads, bones, hands, feet, half-frozen flabby butts. We're all settling together, lumps on lumps, pushing ourselves down into the black tube that will be sealed and dumped into the ocean. The pressure will kill me first, I thought. My ears will go and...

I will not, *will not*, die this way! How? How? How? I have to find some way to break through the plastic, maybe cut it if I can find something sharp. Will it tear? Is it the ripstop stuff? If I had my pen, I could poke it maybe...

I start screaming for help, pushing and shoving against all those bodies—pushing and shoving back. Screaming, screaming, screaming, and my panic returns with a conviction that there's absolutely nothing I can do to help myself, and it's not fair, and somebody should do something, and I hate those bastards who put me and a thousand others in bags...

Okay, breathe, breathe. Slow down and think. What do I have?

Will anything poke through the plastic? It's so dark, so dark. I can't see anything, but I can feel. What do I have?

Something hits me from above. Another body's been slid into the tube.

What's in my pockets? The key to the refrigerator. It's a short cylinder, but it has teeth on the edge. The teeth are small, but maybe they'll work. I grab the key and push it against the plastic opposite my face. It's hard to do with one hand, so I cram my handkerchief into my mouth and suck in the air through it. It tastes terrible and I gag more.

I use the teeth on the key, but the plastic gives and moves, and the surface is slick, so the tiny teeth don't get any bite. I need to push it hard and make the plastic stretch.

The conveyor goes quiet. Enough body bags. Enough bodies. It's time to seal the tube.

I get even more frantic, trying to keep the paralyzing effect of panic from me so I can concentrate. Concentrate! Pushing out doesn't seem to be working. There's just nothing hard to push against—it's all jelly. Even when I find a skull or bone to push against, it slides away.

I pull instead. I use my hands to press against something hard outside the bag, and I'm able to get my fingers to squeeze the plastic together, to pinch a piece of it into a crease that I can pull and finally grab enough to wad up in my hand, giving me something to pull against as I push against it with my elbow. I pull hard and it stretches toward me, letting me jam the ridges of the key into the plastic. I can feel a bite, a small bite, and I try to snag it with an edge and pull it. I need a little opening, that's all.

It slides off, and the key slips out of my hand into the darkness.

Aaarrghhh!

I go back to my pocket to grab my nail clippers. My hands are shaking now, and I'm hearing a different whine outside, but I don't know what it is. I don't want to let go of the wad of plastic I've worked into my fist, so I spit out the handkerchief and use my teeth to open the clipper, fold back the top, and carefully slide it up next to my hand. It's slick, too slick, and my fingers slide off. I fumble the clippers but catch them in time, reposition the jaws, then cram them against the plastic until I've got a small edge that fits between the tiny blades.

It bites. It bites some more. I'm squeezing the lever as fast as I can, and I can feel a hole.

My clippers go back in my pocket, and I push my finger through, stretching the plastic, ripping the hole as big as I can, and suddenly I'm getting more fingers through, then both hands, pulling, pushing, stretching, yanking one hand against the other and I can see dim light and fresh air, and I shove my nose up against it, sniffing in air, then holding my mouth against it, spitting out the noxious taste and gulping in more air while I'm still coughing and gagging.

I vomit again.

I'm pulling and stretching, and I've got leverage enough to move my foot up and use it to stretch the plastic even more. The hole keeps growing.

Pulling the plastic over and around me, I'm out!

I hadn't watched the closing of a deep-sea sausage, but Parker had pointed at the winch above the bag. Two cables hang down, attached to clamps on the side of the sausage. When the operator determines the sausage is full enough, the cables pull the sausage away from the chute and make it more vertical. Two steel bars are then fitted across the tube's opening, and bolts on the bar are inserted through holes in the mouth of the tube to clamp the bars in place, sealing the tube. Forever.

I'm out of the bag, but the sausage suddenly is pulled upright and I fall back into the crowded sacks of bodies—farther from the opening. I scream again and get back up, trying to get my foot on something to step higher on, but the bags keep slipping downward beneath me, sliding from under my feet.

I keep trying, and the lumps and bumps around me finally give me a foothold I can use. I can see the lip of the tube's opening a foot above my upstretched hand. I need more steps, something hard to jump off from to reach up that last foot. I lean down and try to pile up more bags, but it doesn't work—the plastic is too wet from the frost, and they just slide off each other. I try to prop them up as if the people inside were standing, but the bags sag back down.

My panic returns. I'm so close, so close. I'm screaming again. One good push-off is all I need, so I spread my legs and move my feet up and down, packing the bodies closer and pounding them into place, trying to give myself a hard surface to stand. It's like jelly, but maybe hard jelly. Everything is settling. I have to give it a try. I find one body that's fallen over and doubled up. I brace my feet against what feels like a back—and jump. Close. Another try. Closer. The third time, my right-hand grabs the edge. I'm hanging.

But I'm heavy. I can't pull myself up. I need to get my arm

out and hook it over the rim so the operators can't clamp the bar. I see the two metal bars being lowered. A surge of panic gives my right arm the strength of terror and I throw my elbow out the opening and over the edge.

There's a jolt, and the pulley above whines again, but this time, it's in reverse: The tube is being lowered.

———

SEEING an elbow coming out of the tube must have been like seeing Dracula coming out of his coffin. The top operator reversed the pulley to drop the sausage, while the other one climbed up and slipped down the chute to grab my arm. The two of them pulled, and the forklift operator came up to help. Together, they got me out of the chute and down the stairway to an emergency shower station, where they held me as gallons of water dumped all over me. I was coughing, hacking, sneezing, heaving, and screaming from the absolute terror still hammering in my head.

As the water washed over me—my face, my eyes, my mouth, my hands—they stripped off my clothes and rubbed me hard to get the disinfectant off, leaving me violently shaking, naked in the cold. I could do nothing except hold myself up on my hands and knees, and sob as emotions cascaded through me.

The operators were excitedly chattering away at each other. I can't understand a word, but I see one of them speak into a phone. He had to be telling the bridge or Van Thiem of the unbelievable discovery and rescue. Van Thiem and Parker were probably on their way. Okay, I thought, I have no strength to resist, let them come.

Let them be effing surprised that I've come back to haunt them.

An operator gave me a towel, and I finally settled down enough to dry off and pull on a worker's one-piece blue uniform from a storage locker in the corner. I was sliding my feet into a pair of elastic slippers when Van Thiem walked through the door.

CHAPTER 18

I'M EXHAUSTED, but there's enough panic left in me that I slide to the floor and grab onto the leg of the metal table. There's no way I'm letting him put me back into that tube, and I'm sure that's exactly what he wants to do. I'm his big mistake of the day.

I wrap my legs around the table leg, holding on with both hands like a child with a favorite toy, but Van Thiem makes no move toward me. I do nothing more except cower and listen to him jabber at the operators. I have no idea what he's saying, but I'm guessing he's explaining that I'm a derelict visitor trying to commit suicide, that I had snuck into a body bag inside a freezer to cause my own death, and then chickened out. I'm sure he congratulated them on their quick response in saving me and said he'd take it from here.

And, of course, they shouldn't tell anyone it had happened.

Whatever he said, I'm yelling and cursing at them as I'm yanked and twisted and pulled from the table leg and hustled down the corridor, pushed and shoved by Van Thiem, full of hate and plainly furious at my eluding what would have been a thoroughly satisfying death. His mind was probably working through the number of ways he was going to hurt me before he finally, this time, watches me die.

But I've been here before. He's made his biggest mistake: Counting on his previous physical ability to control me, he's left my hands free. As much skulking about as I'd done in the darkness, I knew there were fire extinguishers hanging from each steel rib post separating the bays, and as he keeps his focus down the corridor, I gradually limp, bow, waver, stumble, and suffer toward a post.

When I'm close enough, with a quickness fueled by hate and revenge, in a single motion because I know I'll only get one chance, I grab a fire extinguisher from its hanger, swing it with all my might, and plow it right into the back of Van Thiem's skull.

He dropped like a rock.

I crumpled next to him, breathing hard, joyous at my resolve and aim, but my mind is screaming to get up and get him hidden away. If nothing else, the operators might look this way, and it would be holy hell if my attack was discovered.

Still on my knees, I grab him by the belt and pull him into the darkest recess of the bay. He's wearing cargo pants with multiple pockets, and I quickly empty them onto the floor. One pocket is full of big zip ties, so I cinch his wrists together, then his feet, then use a tie to lash his hands and feet together behind his back. There was a knife in another pocket, so I make strips of his shirt, stuff a strip in his mouth, then fashion a halter around his head to hold the gag in place. I grab his ID necklace, drape it around my neck, pocket his knife, then take off his wristband and wrap it around my own wrist.

Done! Exhausted. With that finished, I half-fall against the bulkhead, incredibly weary and done in.

Now what?

I stumbled up and made for the door. I had to find a way

to get off the ship and back to Oahu. For my sake, for Molly's, and for the opportunity to see Parker Evans fry in an electric chair for his crimes. Escaping from the ship was a question I'd tried to answer before, sitting in my cabin, working my brain hard—with no result. There were only three ways off the ship: the helicopter, the freighter, and the sea boat, the one used to divert big objects floating in the ocean in the platform's path.

I certainly couldn't hide on the ship until a helicopter showed up, or even the next freighter. I couldn't count on the communications, so I couldn't contact anyone. I didn't dare trust any crew members, and I couldn't count on holding anyone hostage until I was rescued because the ship never docked.

That left the sea boat. I needed to get to it, launch it, and get away as soon as possible. I'd have to be gone before the barge crew began their shift for the morning dumping, which was early, like 4:30 or something in the morning.

What time is it now? 2:00, Van Thiem's wristband tells me, and since the body boys were working, it must be the middle of the night. I must have been drugged all day and then bagged for death before the operators started their shift.

I had a little over two hours.

Making it down the corridor and through the large double doors, I focused on the door to Parker's cabin suite. I wasn't going to leave without him, and if I couldn't do that, I'd use Van Thiem's knife to cut the sucker's throat. Call it paranoia about the very rich, but I couldn't save myself, only to find out my childhood friend had taken a sudden helicopter trip to Oahu and jetted from there to some remote country where he'd live happily ever after while an army of lawyers kept the legal system busy for years.

If I had anything to do with it, he would, by God, be either in jail or a cemetery.

CHAPTER 19

Van Thiem's badge gave me access through every door, and I was soon in Parker's cabin suite. Passing by the desks downstairs, I quietly rifled through the drawers, looking for a roll of duct tape—what kind of engineer doesn't have a roll of duct tape?—and stumbled across my cell phone. Of all the miracles—I had my pictures back.

I shoved it in my pocket and kept looking until I found a partial roll of packing tape in a bottom drawer. It wasn't duct tape, but it would do for what I had in mind.

Going upstairs, I found the door to his bedroom on the third try. Parker was sleeping like an angel when I crept next to the bed, put a piece of tape across his mouth, which made him wake up, and then I beat the crap out of him. When we wrestled as young boys, I liked it because I always won, letting him think he had the upper hand and then pouncing on him with my larger frame, laying him flat, and sitting on him until he squealed. The beating I was giving him now was even more unfair. Not only had I given him the first blow when he was barely awake, but every blow afterward was given when he was defenseless.

It was a shameless display of a bully's physical superiority, against everything my father taught me, but I couldn't help pouring out the pent-up rage inside me. I did it for putting me in that damn body bag in that damn tube, for condemning Molly to an agonizing death in the ocean, and for sending all those innocent people to the bottom of the sea. I did it because I couldn't hold back, but I still silently promised him it was only the beginning of the hell I was going to cause him for the rest of his life.

I finally quit, my hands sore and my insides running out of energy, still not feeling like I'd achieved the satisfaction I wanted. The tape had ripped off his mouth, his bottom lip was split and bloody, and his nose had bled down the front of his shirt. His left eye was already swelling, both eyebrows were cut, and red marks on his neck showed where I'd held him as I beat his face. He was unconscious and moaning.

It was time to go. I'd feel sorry for my actions later.

I took his ID necklace from the bedside table and draped it around my neck with Van Thiem's. I threw both their wristbands under the covers of the bed. If someone was tracking the locations of wristbands, it would give them something to talk about. I pulled his cargo pants on him, put him in a new t-shirt, and then slipped a pair of deck shoes on his feet.

Finally, after all these years, being Mutt and Jeff counted for something. I used the packing tape to seal his mouth again, then wrapped his hands against each other behind his back. I wrapped his knees together and his feet, then folded him over my shoulder as I picked him up. I went through those big, beautiful doors and down the stairs, feeling like a pirate who had just captured a king.

The barge was attached to the ship by a grappling system, with two semi-permanent gangways connecting them. The sea boat was in a slip at the barge's stern, and the smaller boat used inside the lagoon was in a slip next to it. Near them was the crane used to close the sausages and bolt the bar across to seal them.

Between the two boat slips was an equipment building for the barge workers. It stored the diving equipment the skirt specialists sometimes used to retrieve submerged objects in the lagoon, a special compressor to refill the air tanks, and accommodations for the workers: a changing room, bathrooms, several shelves of equipment and parts, and large vending machines with both drinks and snacks. It functioned as a break room and provided shelter in case of storms.

I padded toward the equipment building. Parker was squirming, so I propped him up against a railing and used more of the packing tape to strap him down while I inspected the sea boat. Two slings hooked to a motorized winch held both boats up out of the water.

As I moved to the winch, there was a whispered voice behind me, and I froze, imagining Van Thiem magically appearing to put me back in the tube.

"You wouldn't leave without me, would you?"

Molly! I grabbed her, held her, stared at her to make sure she was real. I broke down in tears and refused to let go. I wasn't alone anymore.

How had she escaped?

Talking in a low voice, she told me she was called to Van Thiem's office. When she had entered, he attacked her from behind, gagging her and binding her hands with zip ties behind her back and around her ankles. Then, he unceremoniously carried her to a balcony and dumped her over into the ocean.

"What he didn't know," she said with a small smile, "was that I was on the swim team in college. I couldn't get the ties off, but I held my breath long enough to slip my hands around my butt and get them in front of me. I undid my gag and then dolphin-kicked over close to the ship. I worked my way around to the barge, hopped up the ladder, and found myself a steel support with an edge sharp enough to cut the ties off."

She hid herself during the day under the piping systems near the front, waiting for night so she could search the barge for some way to escape. She had been trying to get one of the boats loose when she saw me.

"There's nothing. There's no way out of here I can find," she said.

I quickly told her what I had found in the containers, yanking out my phone to briefly show her the pictures. I rushed through the conversation with Parker and the fact that he'd confessed he was guilty of having people murdered, and that he'd tried to kill me by drugging me, putting me in a body bag, and tossing me into the deep-sea sausage. I skipped over the gruesome details but told her I'd gotten out and was being taken back to the office by Van Thiem when I whacked him in the head with a fire extinguisher, tied him up, and then kidnapped Parker.

"You did what?" she said as her mouth dropped open.

"I've got Parker. He's coming with us." I led her over to the now-furious man struggling against the railing, gurgling and grunting into the tape across his mouth. He didn't look himself—one eye almost shut, blood caked on his face, bruises dark on his cheeks.

Molly's foot lashed out, the start of a vicious series of kicks into his side. "Son of a bitch!" she screamed. I held her back and reminded her there was no time. "We've got to get that boat going and get to Hawaii."

Struggling out of my hold, she stepped back, and shook her head.

"You didn't hear me. We can't use the boat. It's locked up, and so is the fuel pump."

I grinned and held up Parker's electronic ID card. "Not a problem. I have the power of God."

She looked grim and shook her head again. "The locks aren't electronic. They're real, and I bet the barge master has the only keys."

I didn't believe we couldn't do something. I marched over to the boat, ready to break those locks off by hand if I had to. But she was right, and I was wrong: The lock holding the winch for the boat slings had a protected shank, and it would take a cutting torch to take it apart.

Damn! Damn! Damn!

Molly looked at me with a sorrowful eye. "I didn't find a good way off this boat, but there is another way. You're not going to like it."

She told me.

"You've got to be kidding me," I said, my hopes rising and vanishing in the same instant. "You can *not* be serious!"

CHAPTER 20

THE LOOK on Molly's face showed she wasn't kidding. She didn't like her plan any more than I did, but there was no arguing it was all we had. "Look, we can't use the boats, period, so we're stuck unless we do what I said."

Her plan was to hide in the yellow-ended sausage, let them seal it, release it, and use it as an escape pod until we were dumped out on the ground in Mexico. Absolutely the stupidest idea in the world? Oh, yeah, absolutely! It was a terrible, horrible, awful idea. But there was no time, no time at all.

My hand was shaking as I wiped the sweat off my forehead. *Shit!*

It would be tough enough to escape in a boat, but she wanted to crawl into a damned trash tube? What if we needed to get out? What if the tube was never picked up? What if we ran out of air? How were we going to survive? How could we last until Mexico? What if the tube sank?

Molly grabbed my shaking head and pulled it down close to hers as she looked in my eyes. "There are water bottles in the equipment building, and food. We can take them with us. They pump air into the tube to make sure it floats, so we shouldn't have any trouble breathing. Look at me! It's the only way we can go. It...is...the...only...way."

I felt a wave of hopelessness smothered with fear. Get in the tube? Wasn't there a way to ride on top? Any way we could strap ourselves on without being seen? Could we float next to it, out of sight?

No.

The decision was made. I wasn't sure how much time we had before the barge workers showed up, but it couldn't be more than an hour before the three of us had to be hidden inside. In that time, we had to get the food, water, gear, and whatever else inside the tube—anything that would help us survive for maybe days or even a week. I started shaking again, not believing what I was thinking or imagining was going to happen or what Molly had said or that there were no options and...*shit!*

Running to the equipment building, I ransacked the shelves like I was in Walmart before a hurricane. The diving tanks and respirators plus the dive masks, dive knives, flashlights, packages of batteries, and two handfuls of carabiners. A dozen cartons of shrink-wrapped water bottles stacked next to the soft drink machine, boxes of snacks next to the vending machine—candy bars, granola bars, cookies, chips, and the like—and a first aid kit I yanked off the wall. I grabbed several face respirators, the kind with two filters on the front, which the barge operators used when the wind kicked sludge up into the air, then gloves, small ropes, and three rolls of duct tape, all thrown to Molly, who was shoving everything into mesh bags she'd found on the floor.

"We've got to go," she hissed.

I grabbed three wetsuits and booties off hangers, the biggest I could find for me and two others for Molly and Parker, plus three hard hats, and followed her out the door, carrying as much as I could.

The sausage had a large metal chute across one end, holding the tube open so it could be filled from back to front. It was our luck the tube was already two-thirds full, meaning one more day's dumping of the lagoon would probably fill it enough to be sealed and set afloat.

A soft glow was showing on the horizon as we frantically shuttled our pile of stuff from the equipment building to inside the tube, our arms full each trip. The only light on the barge came from large fluorescents hung from the side of the cruise ship. In the middle of the ocean, across a structure as big as the barge, the effect wasn't much more than a dim nightlight.

The opening of the tube was lighted, but the insides grew darker as we moved deeper into it. We stumbled over piles of trash that had been slung or dragged into the tube by the barge workers: three or four 55-gallon drums full of some-thing, several large pieces of Styrofoam that I recognized as pier floats, old coolers, insulated water jugs, water-logged life jackets, seat cushions, and an unbelievable assortment of other seawater-sodden, smelly, and unrecognizable junk.

Close to where we first entered was a massive tangle of an old fishing net, of what era I couldn't tell, made of heavy twine and twisted rope, full of seaweed and dead fish, with oblong wooden floats around the edges. It had been dragged into the tube and then shoved up over several large mounds of trash. I would never have guessed the net would prove to be one of our greatest assets.

Inside the tube, everything was soaked in sludge-packed seawater, and the floor was sloshing with goop, seaweed, barnacles, and glops of substances I couldn't imagine. We were both gagging as we put on the respirators.

The net seemed our best bet for protection and cushion. I packed enough of it together to make a hollow in the center, then threw the water bottles, snacks, and mesh bags along the sides and folded it back over, creating a cave out of sight from any crew member who might come to the tube's opening. Once we were inside, I would collapse the cave on top of us, shielding us from both discovery and any flying debris. Our immediate need was to stay hidden until the tube was sealed, which I avoided thinking about.

It was time to get Parker. Even with one eye swollen, I'm sure he had been watching us. He knew we were going into the tube, and I'm sure he figured out what that meant. As I used a knife from the equipment building to cut the tape holding him to the railing, he twisted and wiggled and rolled over and gurgled loud moans like he was staring at death. I had trouble holding him down and finally beat him into a half-conscious stupor to get him over to the tube.

I shoved Parker to the very back of our net cave and used five carabiners to hook his taped hands and legs onto several strands of twine. I yanked the tape off his mouth, which woke him, got his attention, put a simple respirator on his face, and then wrapped a circle of tape around it.

"Tear it off and you get to live with the stench," I threatened, leaning close to his ear so he wouldn't miss a word. "And remember this—I don't have a syringe full of whatever you gave me. If you make too much noise, I'll just beat you senseless again.

"You might want to think about that. I guarantee I'll make it hurt."

His eyes took on a new level of fear.

I was hoping no one would notice that the equipment building had been pillaged. On my tour of the barge, Parker had mentioned that equipment was left in a state of readiness at the end of the day in case of an emergency during the night, meaning that everything was prepared for the next day. If nothing was needed from the little building, maybe our burglary would go undiscovered.

Just one day, I was thinking. If we're not discovered today, we can get clear.

We crawled into our fishing net cocoon and pulled the top down not a moment too soon: the metal gangways began squeaking as crew members came down from the Mother Ship. I checked Parker's strappings to make sure they were secure. We had several hours yet, and I absolutely did not want to risk his making a ruckus. He stared silently back at me.

Remember me saying that raising the skirt and dumping the lagoon was a slow process? Try waiting inside a stifling semi-dark cavern of stinky junk with nothing to do but listen, not daring to make any noise or movement that might draw the attention of workers who were not more than twenty yards away. We heard the small motorboat being lowered and started, puttering into the lagoon, the sea boat being winched down and heading out, people talking as it roared into the distance, and banter among the crew members as they went through the ordinary activities of their day. Every now and then, more junk came flying through the chute, adding to the piles around us.

Parker became an immediate problem. When he heard people close, he started flopping around like a fish and yelling at the top of his lungs. I had hoped for different but was expecting it, so I had my hand over his mouth within a couple of seconds. I thought about smothering him to death and getting it over with, but I just took his respirator off, rolled a length of tape into a ball and shoved it in his mouth, taped his mouth again so he was forced to breathe through his swollen nose, then strapped his respirator back on and taped his head to one of the floats. I used the rest of the tape to attach an air tank to his legs and his waist to multiple points of the net. I ran out of tape, but I had accomplished my goal—he had nothing left that moved. If he tried to make guttural sounds or moaned too loud, I slapped him hard on the chest.

I gave no mercy because I had received none. *World view* be damned.

It was a long morning, but we survived—cramped, tired, and fearful of the decision we had made. As the afternoon dumping progressed, someone called out that our tube was full. The chute was pulled away, and the end of the tube was flattened, plunging us into total darkness. We heard the metal strips being positioned and bolted together, sealing the tube and sealing our fate. Molly and I turned on two flashlights, pulled on our wetsuits, stored our clothes in mesh bags, and sat still, hanging onto the net, hoping that it would cushion us from the hundreds of objects we expected would soon be flying around us. I didn't bother trying to get Parker into a wetsuit; he was protected enough.

The sealing was finished, the crane was hooked on, the tube's end was lifted, and we began to slide along the barge. Molly and I interlocked arms and tensed our legs against everything in front of us. I turned off the flashlights and crammed them into my wetsuit, terrified I might lose them.

When all went dark, Parker went into a frenzy—squirming, making noise through his nose, jerking against all the attachments he was hooked to, and making a show of desperate terror beyond anything I'd seen.

Again, I showed no mercy. I wondered how he would have reacted to being in a body bag in a sausage being sent to the bottom of the sea. I wished I had a handful of disinfectant to cram up his swollen nose.

The tube was shoved forward, compressing everything around us as it slipped and slid and turned on the barge floor until it plunged over the lip into the sea. The net intended to anchor us and keep us safe was thrown forward as if it was dropped off a cliff, and we went with it.

In a split second, the contents of the tube exploded into chaos.

The front end hit the water, throwing everything forward, then jerking as the back end slapped against the water. The tube bobbed up and down end-to-end, rolled over several full rotations—insides mashing and crunching and pressing together as if in a giant washing machine—while the sludge, seawater, goop, and guck that had collected on the bottom was now slung and flung over, on, and around us. We were repeatedly thrown head over heels and pummeled by trash that mashed us, beat us head to toe, and snagged our wetsuits, our bags, our hands, our everything. We could do nothing but grab the hard hats, cram them on tight, and burrow ourselves farther into the net.

Churning in the ocean swells, I turned on a flashlight and gave it to Molly as I cut the tape holding Parker's legs to the air tank and his head to the net, afraid he might be torn apart if the tank broke free from the net. I strapped his hard hat on, hoping it wasn't too late—it would do us no good if he was injured. Judging from the guttural sounds coming through his respirator, he was screaming like the rest of us, so at least he wasn't dead.

The ocean worked us over as the tube rolled up and down in the water, now turning into alignment, then swinging wildly, madly upsetting everything around us. The three of us hung desperately to the net as we jerked back and forth, up, down, and sideways, until the fierce random forces tore it loose and wiped out any pretense of an anchor or safe cocoon.

Who knows how many minutes shot by, but the sausage finally settled. The metal drums acted like ballast in the bottom of the tube, with loose trash all around them, and the upper half of the tube was a landscape of bulky items sticking out of the jumble.

Seasickness came in waves, then passed. Molly and I

turned on more flashlights, then scrambled to pull the old fishing net out of the confusion. Shifting what we could, pulling off the fish carcasses, barnacles, and seaweed, tossing everything we didn't want in front of us, we recreated an opening and threw the net over it, hooking it on whatever corners and crimps we could and restoring the cushion we had first hoped for.

We wiped the crap off ourselves and our respirators, and gathered the bags of equipment, water, food, and air tanks. We searched frantically until we found another roll of duct tape to repair the tears, snags, and cuts our wetsuits had suffered. I cut the rest of the tape holding Parker to the net, unhooked the carabiners, and cut his legs and hands loose. There was now no escape for him. He had become our equal, needing to use his hands, legs, and body to defend himself against the tube's constant churning. With his hands free, he yanked off his respirator, spit out the wad of tape, and laid into us with as vile a stream of language as I'd ever heard.

I slapped him hard enough to send him reeling back into the net.

"Let's get some things straight, you son of a bitch. We're equals in here, except I'm a hell of a lot more equal than you. I'll give you one minute to get out all the shit you want to say, but then the three of us are going to act civilly toward each other, got it? If you don't, then by God, I'll tape you up like a mummy. Now, I brought you a wetsuit," I said as I threw the last one at him. "Put it on because it's going to get cold, and you're going to need it to keep warm. Keep your hard hat on, keep your respirator on, and hold onto the net. We're all in the same boat, so behave."

He spent a few more minutes cursing, then refused to sit in the nest we had made. He tunneled forward, grabbing his wetsuit, respirator, and hard hat, and found a place in the darkness ahead of us.

Molly and I turned off the flashlights.

Parker's voice was suddenly quivering, screaming commands, then asking, then begging for a light to be turned back on. I turned the light on, and he started the cursing again. I shut it off, and he was back to sniveling and begging.

What do you know? The two-time Nobel Prize winner, king of the ocean's trash, and serial murderer of the homeless is scared of the dark.

"I told you to be civil, Parker," I called into the darkness, "and I now have a new negotiating tool. Act like the jerk you are, and you're doomed to darkness. Treat us better and we'll keep the light on at least until we figure out how long it'll last. Deal?"

"We don't have enough batteries to leave a flashlight on," Molly shouted through her respirator. "Let him suffer!"

I didn't mind beating Parker, but mentally torturing anybody is something I can't do. Besides, we all have our personal demons, and letting any of them out inside this tube was not a good idea.

"We'll figure how much light we can have later. Right now, I want him to obey."

A voice squeaked in the darkness, and I turned the light back on. In the dim light, I watched as he crawled back to us, his eyes wide open, clearly frightened to the bone. He inserted himself back into the net, took off his shirt and pants and stuck them in a mesh bag, pulled on his wetsuit, refitted his respirator and hard hat, and settled in next to me.

"I expect my own flashlight," he said with a thinly disguised snarl.

I ignored him. I wasn't about to give up my leverage.

Barely withstanding the punishment being doled out by a sea that did not suffer fools, the three of us settled ourselves into the net, wrapped our hands into its weave, pushed our feet into the pile of bags below us until we were braced, and held on as the sausage rocked and rolled in the waves. Even Parker kept himself anchored, finally accepting that none of us had either power or control.

It was the beginning of days of darkness, loneliness, choking air, constant jarring movement, and consuming fear, and, yes, it had been a terrible, horrible, awful idea.

CHAPTER 21

I'VE READ about the Apollo astronauts during the long flights to the moon. Their capsule was considerably smaller than our sausage, but they had lights, voices, clean air, windows, and things to do. They slept at certain times, woke at certain times, and had specific and well-rehearsed activities that occupied a good part of every single day—constantly monitoring the condition of the space capsule and performing a myriad of other duties. The activities were not arbitrary. In planning the missions, NASA developed libraries of information about how people acted and reacted during long periods of isolation, like space travel, and designed every facet of the capsule environment to keep the astronauts emotionally stable, competent, healthy, and feeling safe.

There was nothing safe about our tube.

The simple act of inhaling was hard. The air in the tube was barely breathable. It stank to the level of gagging, and the constant churning kept the odors fresh and repugnant, forcing us to continually wear the respirators. They failed miserably whenever the tube was violently rolled or upended, drenching the air with a horribly tasting stench and soaking the filters until they were useless. When we could feel it coming, we learned to yank off the respirators, cram them in our wetsuits, and strap on the diving respirators and dive masks so we could breathe from the air tanks. It made a bad situation tolerable.

Molly calculated how long our air would last. I hadn't thought about it—we were in a forty-foot sausage that was eight feet in diameter. It seemed cavernous, so I assumed there'd be enough air no matter how long we were trapped. But as she described the parameters—the volume of air in the tube, the percentage of space taken up by the junk, the amount of oxygen the three of us were replacing with carbon dioxide—it began to feel important.

I helped her out with data I'd learned from scuba diving, like respiration rates, efficiency of oxygen consumption, and such, but then she got into how long we'd be in the tube: How quickly would we be yanked out of the sea by the collection ship? Once we were yanked out of the sea, how long before we made it to Mexico? Once we made it to Mexico, how long before the sausage would be emptied?

She drilled into my head that the air in the tube was finite and at some point, there'd be none left. I quizzed Parker as to the timing of the sausage operation, but he was amazingly ignorant about the numbers Molly needed. He had long been out of the daily business of the collection ships and the operations in Mexico and had no clue about the lengths of time between transfers. That made me the resident expert, so I best-guessed what she needed. I was intentionally optimistic. We were in it for the duration, and worrying about running out of air was something we didn't need.

Using my numbers, Molly determined we'd be okay if we avoided using the air tanks except for catastrophic events. But there'd only be enough for the two of us—we'd have to kill Parker.

"Really?" I asked skeptically.

"Well, okay, we don't have to kill him, but he can only take a breath every other minute," she replied.

I found myself laughing—it seemed unreal—but her disrespect for the man ruled all her thoughts and feelings. Every time his feet slid over to her side of the net, she'd call him an asshole and give them a kick, which kept me sitting between the two of them.

"You know," I told her, "we may be together a long time. Give him some slack. At least I'm not threatening to use duct tape on you. Now, do we have enough air to make it?"

She huffed. "Yeah, we should have no problem. But don't expect me to share the last tank with him if it comes down to that. If we're going to die, I'm going to watch him do it first."

I agreed with her just to keep the peace. I didn't ask what would happen if she had to share the last tank with me.

Molly did the same math with the water, knowing it was critical that we stay hydrated. There was plenty, she figured, and suggested we each drink four bottles a day.

She was cool and collected as she churned through the calculations in her head, and I was even more impressed. The Montana Ranch Girl had grit as well as strength. I was glad. It was going to take a lot of both to get us into the sunshine of Mexico. I was going to need her. I'd never been the hero type. I lived by communicating, not leading, and I was already feeling sick from the stress.

Should we ration the snacks? We decided that food wasn't that important—people can survive for a long time without food, and we had what seemed like plenty of snacks—not that the body does very well on a corn-chip-and-peanut diet, but our ultimate survival wouldn't depend on food. We decided on a restricted, but constant schedule. When everything was gone, we'd just be hungry. Compared with all the other shit we were in for, hunger didn't rate very high.

Dealing with bathroom needs seemed manageable.

Because of the humidity, we were going to be sweating buckets, even in wetsuits in the cold air, so we probably wouldn't pee much. We certainly weren't going to eat much, so pooping wouldn't be a big problem, although constipation might be. The opposite end of the tube from our net was the obvious place for bathroom functions. I would like to say, just for the record, that the smell of urine is surprisingly unique. We were already surrounded by a high level of stench, but the addition to it when one of us peed was never missed.

Measuring time was what we missed first, especially Parker. None of us had watches, but of course, our internal clocks were calibrated to normal twenty-four-hour cycles. The first day, we talked about time, referred to time, measured ourselves by time, and expected our actions to vary by time. When we should drink, how long since we drank last, how long till we'd drink next, when we should eat, and especially when we should expect to sleep and for how long.

I bet we were hours off within the first day. Having the correct time didn't really matter, so we ultimately let our expectations go. We ate when hungry—although we all ate the same things at the same time—drank when thirsty, or at least regularly, and slept when we could, which was never more than drifting off for a few minutes.

That left the darkness. It was the demon of all of us.

I found the mesh bag with the battery packs. I had grabbed five flashlights from a shelf and found seven shrink-wrapped packages of ten batteries each. Parker still wanted his own light, which I understood, but he demanded having it on all the time.

Molly tried figuring out how many days of light power we had, but we didn't have enough data. I finally loaded one up with new batteries and gave it to Parker, since I knew he'd keep it on until it died. It lasted what we thought was half a day. Surely, we agreed, we would be dumped out in Mexico in less than a month, so with seventy batteries, we decided to leave one flashlight on all the time, and Parker could hold it.

It was a foolish decision, but not for the reason you're thinking.

With the light on, we felt better, but there were more demons in the shadows than Parker's single flashlight revealed, the first being that the barely lit tube created a two-dimensional world that blunted our brains' ability to sort out our environment. Something would fall or shift or slide into us, startling us with no warning and no way of knowing if the event was over or if that was just the start. When big waves suddenly rolled us, the bouncing light was more disorienting than pure darkness, like being inside a kaleidoscope. If we lost our grip and tumbled around, we scrambled with three flashlights to get back to the safety of the net. When the net itself was jerked loose, we crashed into what seemed like every piece of trash in the tube, and took even more flashlight time to sort out and reposition ourselves.

The second problem was that having only one light drove us to fear losing all our light. I kept reminding Molly and Parker that we had plenty of flashlights and batteries, but it didn't dull the growing fear—even for me—that we might lose all the light we had. We grew more concerned about future darkness than we were about present darkness. Especially Parker, who was becoming more withdrawn and protective of his flashlight. He would cuddle it and hold it close, blocking the light from Molly and me and making our world even darker.

He had already been keeping as far away as he could, if only by a matter of inches, but he was adamant about being untouched and uncomforted. He still ate, still drank, and still responded if we asked him a question, but he seemed not to care a whit when Molly and I were talking to keep our spirits up.

I saw an ancient prison cell in Italy once. It was nothing more than a room deep in a castle, with an immense stone floor, stone walls and a curved stone ceiling. I was too tall to stand up. No benches, no beds, no desks, no windows, no anything. A bucket for waste that might or might not be emptied on any given day. A prisoner had nothing—absolutely nothing—to do and no place to go. Imagine being chained to the wall.

Prisoners often went mad.

Parker was far from being that bad, all things considered, but he seemed to feel no need for a survival strategy. He reacted to everything with the same level of blind panic. Perhaps he had faith in an impending escape regardless of what we did, but I doubted it.

Whether it was his anger at us or his disorientation or his fear, he remained distant, accepting whatever was suggested or what he was directed to do, or, in the aftermath of being rolled or crashed, helping by doing what was required when he was told to. He would then curl back up in the net, cuddling his flashlight, wiping the crap off his hands, face, and head, and stubbornly staring ahead of him as if the other two of us didn't exist.

Not that I lost my hate for Parker and all he had done to me and others, but it was discouraging to see someone refuse to do what seemed necessary for maintaining hope. It was as if he had never had to face being alone before and didn't know how destructive loneliness could be.

For Molly and me, it was the opposite approach, our hands or our thighs touching as we moved, wetsuit brushing wetsuit, not for passion or out of fear but for orientation and the conscious assurance that we were not alone. It made it easier to accept the darkness.

For us, talking was a survival tool. The difference in our ages slipped away. The subject didn't matter. We could have recited the alphabet and it would have been comforting. Being a newspaperman, though, I had a million and one facts and stories, and I was unabashed about piling on the details, while Molly listened. It made me feel heroic, which was new to me.

Touching gave us a defined space, a beginning and an end, and talking gave us the three dimensions that the tyranny of the dark denied us. The net we wrapped around our bodies when the tossing was intense, serving as our constant point of reference. If it didn't offer quite the comfort of a mother's womb, it still made a protective nest.

My old body obviously suffered more every time a big wave reshuffled our space. Molly was made of more resilient stuff, coming back quicker after being rocked and rolled while I struggled to crawl back to the net each time, every joint aching and every bone feeling whacked. When I'd regained my place, touching Molly's hand or arm was the first thing I did. She hadn't asked for protection, but I was the one who needed it.

———

WE HAD CRAWLED into the yellow-ended sausage in the early morning and been dumped in the Pacific that afternoon. It was two days later, we guessed, when we were snatched from the ocean.

Being picked up by the collection ship was less traumatic than being dropped off at the end of the barge, but the sausage still rolled over at least twice as it was being stored onboard, tumbling us and our homey little world back into chaos. We held on as best we could to the net and air tanks, clenching our teeth around the respirator mouthpieces. Listening to the noise of chains and winches and feeling the grinds and bumps, we pictured our tube being hooked onto a cable, lifted up, and pulled across a long metal floor, then stacked in the ship's huge bay.

After that, there was no more wave action, no more bobbing up and down, no more chaotic movements from weather and ocean that had savaged our escape pod. It was a dramatic change physically but incredibly more important, mentally. We had lasted through the first step and reached the first milestone. We would never again be floating on the ocean, and our fears of the sausage ripping apart, being caught in a typhoon, or countless other horrors condemning us to drift forever until we died a slow and miserable death, were now only memories.

After setting our topsy-turvy house in order, each of us, Parker included, celebrated with a bottle of water and a chocolate bar.

Then it was time to sleep.

Knowing I was about to collapse, I feared what Parker might do if both Molly and I were asleep. But there was no choice. I grabbed a mesh bag, tossed in the knives, and hooked it into the net between Molly and me, then half-laid against it.

I was out in seconds.

The chaotic travel for two days in the open ocean had kept all of us from any real sleep. It had been too rough, too unpredictable, with no stability to let us sit or lie down long enough to pass out for more than a few minutes. By the time the sausage was pulled onto the collection ship, we were all in an exhausted stupor. Even Parker, who had done little more than huddle in a fetal position with his flashlight, was shaking from raw nerves.

How long did we sleep? I don't know. Did we wake up refreshed? No. We woke feeling something between being hung over and dead. We ached from the lack of real cushioning, felt queasy from the lack of motion, had headaches and body aches far beyond the help of the few pain pills in the first aid kit, were bathed in sweat from our wetsuits, and continually suffered the nastiness coating our bodies.

But we had more light!

Wait a minute. Why did we have more light?

Parker.

Apparently, the only thing he did as Molly and I slept was to steal the five flashlights, cuddle them in his arms—all turned on—and then fallen asleep with the spare batteries stashed beneath him. Coming slowly out of my grogginess, I yanked four of them away and turned them off while he kept snoozing like a baby. I didn't realize he had also stolen the extra batteries.

Molly was startled out of her sleep soon afterward, plainly frightened by a racing brain. Parker slept for maybe another hour.

Without asking, I took two bottles of water, stripped off my wetsuit, gave my hair and face a hand bath, then squirted myself all over. I could tell I was pretty rank. Liberating my private parts, rubbing all those places covered by neoprene, and then scrubbing my hands and head was like being at a luxury spa, and I loved every moment of it.

What I would have given for a bar of soap. Irish Spring—oh, yeah!—one of those bars with a really strong scent to battle the awful smell that was me and everything else.

After I was finished, Molly grabbed two bottles and did the same, unabashedly peeling everything off in the weak light of Parker's flashlight.

I tried not to be foolish, but I didn't look away either. Her full breasts, flat stomach, muscled legs and ass—I wasn't thinking much about our plight at that moment. Yes, I'd gotten a glimpse through her pajamas top, a better view in her swimsuit, and now there was nothing between those nipples and me. Perched on the edge of hell, I felt like I'd never seen breasts before.

I retrieved our clothes from the mesh bag and enjoyed the feel of cotton against my skin even though it was a blue jump-suit like the mechanical room operators used. My dad had worn one forty years ago, and I'd sworn never to even have one in my closet. I handed Molly her clothes from the bag, avoiding her eyes, but I could see she had a sheepish grin.

When Parker woke and learned of our baths, he did the same. I didn't watch, and I'm sure Molly didn't either.

We had crossed a new boundary in our journey.

CHAPTER 22

GETTING the clothes out of the bag revealed that the batteries had been stolen. There was no doubt who was guilty. Parker had not only taken the batteries, he had also torn off the packaging and shoved the individual batteries under himself like a king sitting on bars of gold. All those loose batteries had then dropped through the weave of the net into an uncountable number of dark, narrow, squishy crevices running the entire length of the tube. When I yanked him out of his seat, I could find only ten.

It was my turn to lash out with all my pent-up anger, yelling vile names, insulting his parents, degrading his Nobel prizes, jabbing him with my finger, slapping him on the chest and arm. Molly flamed even hotter. I had to fight to keep her from strangling him.

Parker merely sat there cowering and smirking.

Afterwards, we forced him to work with us at finding the batteries, moving the net around, tunneling through mounds of trash, pushing our hands into all sorts of slime, and finally giving up with only fifty-one batteries out of the seventy we'd counted on.

We had lost more than a fourth of our potential light.

It was senseless, and I was ready to tape Parker spread-eagled over a 55-gallon drum, but it would have done no good: He seemed unperturbed by the gravity of what he had done. I considered taking away his flashlight as punishment, but the pleasure of hurting him would have led only to his constant screaming as the darkness tormented him.

I wondered if he was losing his grip on reality. In addition to his lack of remorse, he had stopped looking normal. He didn't stand and move around anymore, content with merely slouching in the net. He kept tilting his head, as if it had grown too heavy, sometimes rocking it from side to side. He slept whenever he wanted, without regard to anything else going on, and spoke to us in grunts instead of sentences.

Still quaking with anger and hostility, I gave myself an assignment to focus on. Without the fear of water rushing in, I grabbed a dive knife and a flashlight and attacked the fabric of our prison. I tried poking, stabbing, slicing, shaving, drilling—whatever I could think of—but after an hour, I'd managed only a scratch. It was like using the blade on steel.

"You'll never penetrate it," Parker said loudly, though his voice was muffled by his respirator. "I made it indestructible. You see, it's all about aligning the molecules in a dense geometric pattern with nanoscale manipulation." He kept going, still loudly, explaining the material's atomic structure, single atom layering on substrates, nanoscale chemistry, wrapping ion charges, and stuff I'd never heard of. He was soon standing, lecturing, even waving his arms as if drawing graphs on a chalkboard.

An hour later, he was into a full-blown explanation of polymer science.

Well, okay, let him go until he runs out of steam. It was better than the seething silence. He wasn't addressing me in particular, or anyone in particular for that matter, so I kept on working on the tube's wall. When Parker got deep into explaining a series of equations, Molly threw her hands up and grabbed her own knife and flashlight. She was more patient than me, but it made no greater difference. At least we had something to do.

Remember the astronauts preserving their schedule and constant activities?

In the open ocean, the swells and current had made every minute a battle against an all-consuming foe that wreaked havoc against any sort of orderly environment we tried to construct. Repeating the cleanup routine kept us grounded in our reality, however small it was, and then it was back into the net to hold on tight until the next round of chaos.

Now, layered in the collection ship with other sausages, the war was over, and our regular routine no longer protected us. As soon as our escape pod was captured and dragged into place, we turned on our lights, shuffled everything back into order, redistributed the trash that had shifted, straightened up the net and our bags, and recreated our living quarters, just as we had done before. Now, however, it no longer changed, robbing us of mission duties. We had gone from battling a phantom of war to babysitting a ghost of idleness and boredom.

Our routine became simple: We did nothing except breathe, occasionally sleep, occasionally eat, occasionally drink, and occasionally pee. We had more time to think, more time to worry, more time to fear the future, and more time to notice the darkness.

———

ON AUGUST 5, 2010, near Copiapo, Chile, a block of stone as tall as a forty-five-story building broke away from inside the upper part of a mountain and dropped onto the miles of tunnels of a copper and gold mine snaking through the mountain beneath it.

That block of stone sealed off every passage out of the mine, and the thirty-three men inside found themselves trapped in an emergency shelter twenty-three hundred feet below ground. That's a half-mile of solid rock between them and the outside world.

It was seventy days before they were rescued.

In addition to the small shelter, the men had more than a mile of tunnels to move around in, and access to various pieces of mining equipment. They used a backhoe to dig for water, and drained the radiators of other machines for liquid to drink. The ill-stocked emergency supplies in the shelter had been meant for two or three days, but were rationed for two weeks, the men consuming two spoonfuls of tuna, a sip of milk, and a biscuit every forty-eight hours, sometimes adding a morsel of peach. They used truck batteries to recharge their hard hat lamps, and periodically turned on vehicle lights to simulate daytime.

Seventy days. What did those miners do for seventy days?

The people above ground were working furiously without even knowing if any miners were alive, drilling multiple shafts to reach passageways or shelters that might have given them refuge. It took seventeen days before they were success-ful, finally pulling out a drill bit with a message tied on the end, telling them that thirty-three men below wanted to live. For seventeen days, those men had existed without contact with the outside world.

After the drill shaft found them and communications were established, the men below were given food, water, air, elec-tricity, and media screens, but they still had fifty-three more days of loneliness and boredom before they were brought up through an innovative one-person capsule lowered through a large, specially drilled shaft.

The final rescue operation was televised live, supposedly watched by a billion people worldwide.

Seventy days.

I was pretty sure we had less than seventy days before rescue, but would we survive the time we did have? What had Beth, my wife, done when I didn't return? Had she called the police or the Coast Guard, or Parker's corporation? I would bet she'd called my editor, and that the two of them were feverishly trying to find out what had happened to me. Had Parker's disappearance been reported? What had Van Thiem done? I couldn't believe anyone would have thought of us escaping in a sausage, so they must have assumed we were hiding somewhere on the ship.

How long had the crew searched bow to stern for us? How long did it take to find Parker's wristband and realize he was missing, too?

How long before the world knew? If Parker was missing, stock markets all over the world would have been jolted, so I had to believe someone would have demanded an investigation. But I had no idea what really was going on. No contact with the outside world meant all I could do was wonder.

Once the three of us had finally gotten some sleep, had our ceremonial baths, and straightened our house, we took stock of the supplies. We sorted our food into one bag—a variety of packaged cookies, chips, candy bars, peanut butter and crackers, packages of peanuts with chocolate bits, trail mix, mixed nuts, and three boxes of chewing gum. We put our sundries into another bag—what was left of the batteries, the knives, the duct tape, rope, clothing—and our wetsuits, scraped clean and patched, into a third bag. We then stacked our plastic-wrapped bottles of water next to the tube wall, wrapping them with duct tape to keep them together.

Was it enough? How many days would we spend in this makeshift emergency shelter before we got to Mexico? Would we be insane when we got there, or would God be merciful and let us die first?

The Chilean miners were almost all Catholic and prayed daily as a group, and many said their faith had sustained them. They formed teams and took on work assignments but also adopted a *one man, one vote* system for solving problems and keeping order. Their democracy was important, they said afterward. Their leader, a common man of uncommon strength and purpose, orchestrated their daily lives and ultimately cared for every single person under his charge. His actions sustained them.

We had one older man, one strong woman, and one Nobel Prize winner who refused to socialize, a snack machine's worth of marginal food, water, flashlights, batteries, and a growing team of demons that constantly and incessantly occupied our minds—darkness, silence, and time. It wasn't looking good.

Molly was asleep when she had her first panic attack. Crouched in the fishing net next to her in our muted darkness, I heard her breathing increase, then felt her body twitch.

"Are you still with us?" I asked.

She began gulping in air, then yanked off her respirator. "Aaahhhhh…" she started to yell, gasping and crying out in terror. Soon, she was screaming at the top of her lungs.

I grabbed her, but she pushed me away, screaming like a banshee.

Parker began laughing as he suddenly sat up and turned his light on her. I didn't know what to do but tried touching her with my feet as I held my hands over my ears.

"Eeeee…" Molly screamed, wailing at full volume, then stopping to take in large gulps of air. "Aahhhhh…"

She soon exhausted herself, and I felt the net give as she

collapsed into a fetal position, moaning, cursing, her voice filled with frustration and fear and hate. Her chest heaved at the exertion, and soon she was crying uncontrollably.

I tried to hold her, but she pushed me away again, violently shoving me across the net.

"Don't touch me! Leave me alone!" she wailed.

I did nothing. I could only grieve in silence. Was she dying? What if I lost her?

It was our first lesson in blind despair. Sometimes, no matter what, your heroic internal defenses against darkness and silence will fail, and you will plunge into utter hopelessness. It's not your fault, and it's not yours to control. It's part of being an animal with a sophisticated brain that has been trained to be hopeful, positive, and optimistic, and when that training fails, your physical body has to react, and that's when you spiral into despair.

An hour after she settled down, Molly and I talked about setting rules to handle ourselves, with me deliberately looking at Parker as I spoke, believing that if his behavior continued to worsen, he might succumb to an attack next. We agreed to a screaming protocol: Any one of us could scream anytime we wanted or needed to, there would be no touching or holding, and certainly no words of comfort. Afterward, each of us was to wait at least ten minutes before putting our feet together, but then we were *required* to put our feet together. There would be no holding or comforting until later, and only when the screamer voluntarily agreed, and anything said during a screaming session was not to be remembered.

"I'll say bad things," Molly said, "things I won't mean. I just have to get them out of me."

"I agree to not remember and to not think badly of you, or myself," I said in return.

Parker had no reaction.

Most important to our protocol, we would not speak platitudes or offer empty comfort. It was better to be silent and let the rawness flood in. There was nothing she or I could say in those moments that would feel true. We knew it would all sound false and hollow.

At other times, we could be encouraging and comforting but not during a scream session. When that happened, we were too sensitive to dishonesty.

The two of us had other agreements. We talked about despair, wanting to give up, and the depression because of the pervading darkness. We talked about dying, since it seemed inevitable. We forced ourselves to admit our complete lack of control, even though it was the opposite of how we both had been raised and trained. We agreed to discuss these things but to keep our therapy sessions short.

We had a rule against insulting each other: We did not ever, especially in anger, put each other down—and that, with me forcing the issue, included Parker. I would say nothing about her decision to escape via the sausage, and she would ignore my need to confront Parker, which had gotten us into this situation in the first place. We did not talk about Parker, Van Thiem, or the horror of dumping innocent homeless people into the sea. That would have only stirred up hate, and if we were to die, we did not want our last thoughts to be of hate.

All of our openness and confessions of weakness took its toll on my mind. I missed the close intimacy of a companion, and I had to fight to keep from grabbing Molly and holding her body tight against my own. The feelings weren't totally sexual, but being so close for so long under such conditions had confused my emotions: I would have liked to break down and cry on her shoulder as much as I would have liked to fondle her breasts.

Being so lonely, so isolated, and so vulnerable robbed me

of my feeling for privacy, and I watched for any small indication she might have similar feelings.

No indication ever came, and I kept my hands to myself.

A damned fool was what I was, thinking about her that way in the first place. Molly and I had been combatants in war, and we were now combatants in suffering. We were way past the realm of friendly bonding. There was no relief from fear, no moments of inner peace, no relaxed moments of reflection, no family settings, no forgetting how much we craved being set free, and if it didn't make us better friends, it made us better survivors. If we were forming bonds, they bypassed our hearts and directly connected our guts. Any show of passion would have been a mistake, and I was glad I resisted.

Molly and I went back to a regular schedule of work, like the astronauts a million miles out in space and those miners buried deep in the earth. Even if it didn't need it, we straightened our nest. We rearranged the air tanks and other equipment, set out our dive bags and went through them in an orderly fashion, and reorganized our water bottles. Whatever it took to be busy.

What was Parker doing during all this? He was becoming more worrisome.

I had once interviewed inmates at a local prison. For most of them, anger, disillusionment with our justice system, or hatred for other people kept them mentally alert, and usually dangerous, but there were some who would only withdraw into their own world. Perhaps it was loss of hope, perhaps they had no tools to cope. Maybe it was emptiness or despair, or maybe it was the voices only they could hear.

This was the category Parker was clearly moving into. He began talking to himself. Quietly, intellectually, articulately, but nonetheless, only to himself. Usually, it was a lecture or an explanation of some physical process, or a discourse on some international problem he'd addressed in the past. Whatever it was, it kept him occupied, and for that, Molly and I were thankful. We were content to let him be.

That's how we spent our time on the collection ship. That's how we made it from one period of being alive to another period of being alive.

CHAPTER 23

SOMETIMES, we could hear a loudspeaker, bells, whistles, and a booming fog horn. It drove us crazy to think that we were so close to people, so close to freedom, so close to food, fresh air, showers, and soft beds. And sunlight, blessed sunlight.

When we heard anyone, we screamed to no avail. We covered our ears, and I beat an SOS on the big steel drums. It would leave us breathless and elated when we thought it might have worked, and crushed when we knew it hadn't.

It had seemed like forever when we finally felt the ship slow, then stop. We hustled getting things ready, putting on our wetsuits, getting our tanks and respirators, lashing things down even more. We were ready to be one more step away from freedom—one more hurdle before we were released to rejoin a normal world.

The unloading of the sausage beat the devil out of us, since we had been lulled into forgetting what it was like. We heard a line being hooked onto our front, felt the tube being pulled across the steel bay of the collection ship, which made it roll a couple of times, and then we crashed down into a heap as the tube was jerked upright. It dangled for a few minutes and then was dropped onto a conveyor belt like a wrestler throwing an opponent to the mat. There was a small yank as we were disconnected.

We were bruised, battered, and sore, and had more punctures and rips to our wetsuits as well as cuts on our arms and legs. We let the tension release, breathed deeply from our tanks, turned on the flashlights—Parker had not turned his off—and switched back to the smaller face respirators. Molly and I immediately began housekeeping, almost with glee, shoving and lifting and throwing stuff around to restore our net to a livable position.

We were on solid ground—no more ocean, no more waves, no more seasickness. We stripped off our wetsuits, took not-so-ceremonious baths, reestablished our nest, then cleaned and patched the wetsuits, swearing to never do it again. It made us feel like there was truly going to be an end to our journey.

How long until our tube would be taken to the drying floors and emptied? We were discussing possible timeframes when we realized that something had crept out of the darkness and surrounded us.

The heat.

Why did Parker Evans locate his drying floors in remote, sunny locations? To expose the trash to the sun's intense and unrelenting heat to eke out every bit of moisture.

We were now under that same sun—in a mostly black, sealed container.

How long?

I couldn't remember the average time from when a sausage offloaded from a ship was emptied on a drying floor. Perhaps I hadn't been told, but it had to depend on the number of sausages coming in and the rate of drying, so locations along the runways came open as the trash was gathered and removed. I might ask later, I told myself, to have the number in case it was ever needed.

But when we started baking to death, I knew it was never going to be needed.

Every few days in the summer, my newspaper ran articles from the Associated Press about a baby or small child dying in a hot car somewhere, left there as Mom or Dad dashed into the store for a minute or two—or maybe even forgot a child was in their back seat.

A car with an air conditioner can be sixty degrees inside as it's being driven all over town but when turned off under a hot sun, the inside air will heat to over 130 degrees in a matter of minutes.

As our tube kept heating up, we doused our heads with water from our remaining bottles. Not because we were dry—the humidity had always been a problem, and with the added heat, we were now living in a sauna. We even took some of the goop and smeared it on our arms and legs. Anything to fend off the heat.

How long?

I don't know. We had tried to count the number of sausages being taken from the collection ship and lowered onto the conveyor belt, but the sounds were confusing. Knowing would have told us how far back in line we were— the fewer tubes ahead of us, the faster we would be lifted and spilled out. We had no idea how fast the conveyor moved or how regimented the time might be. Did they work only until the workers went home? Were the tubes distributed during the night to be ready in the morning?

How long, how long, how long?

The heat built quickly. We tried to focus on the conveyor belt jerking and jolting us along but soon could think of nothing but the heat. Then our last light went out.

Parker had lost several batteries, we'd used more trying to cut through the tube, others were lost during every chaotic upset, and we had burned through handfuls during our days on the collection ship.

Too many, I guess, but I had, quite frankly, neglected to keep track.

As the last flashlight dimmed, the demon of darkness returned, but it came quietly this time, almost with sadness, because Molly and I had no energy to oppose it, and Parker had already gone to a place where it no longer mattered.

Remember the prisoners I talked about, the ones who withdrew into a place of their own? When it was coming, the other inmates knew, and even the hardcore among them understood that the crazies should be left alone, even pitied.

Parker gave no sound when his flashlight dimmed to nothing. He'd been told there were no more batteries and there would be no more light. Feeling the net move, I knew he had turned away and retreated deeper into his corner. I had no pity and yelled at him in the darkness for what he had brought us to. I knew it didn't matter to him, and it didn't even matter to me. Yelling was just something I could do, and the things I could do were getting fewer and fewer.

Molly and I were now alone in the darkness. We felt dizzy, sick, and when I touched my arms, I felt only the now-gummy goop. Throwing away the trash around them, we hugged the steel drums to capture any coolness, but even they were slowly heating up.

I was so, so sorry, and began blubbering in the darkness. Such a young, vibrant, strong woman, and she was going to die. So much more life to live, and I was going to die. It wasn't right.

Those trapped miners in Chile? The first video made by lowering a camera down the drill hole showed each of them shirtless and glistening: It was 104 degrees and 98 percent humidity.

We would have been happy to be so cool. The minutes

passed, and we could do no more. We no longer noticed when our conveyor belt started and stopped as the tubes in front of us were lifted away by the distribution cranes.

Have you ever wondered what you would do if you knew you were dying? I watched my father and mother slowly suffer and die, separated by twenty-four years. I've read countless obituaries of people dying after long illnesses, too often, and I've seen the suffering that precedes a heart giving up.

I had always thought my death would be like those— suffering a long time and then slowly drifting away. Now, death coming would be a relief. Inside my tube prison, I had suffered and all those uncountable minutes were counted against my mortal clock. But before the unending heat, I had stood against the suffering because I expected to live. Now, my suffering was not to live—I had given up on that—but was only to delay my death.

I don't think you can understand. The heat hurt so terribly. I just wanted it all to be over.

Strength dissolves into weakness, resolve becomes resignation, and life becomes death.

Hardly able to draw air from the tank-connected respirators, hardly mentally aware, our bodies aching for a taste of cool water, Molly and I leaned back into our fishing net, placed our sweaty, sludge-covered hands together and gave up hope. All we had worked for, all we had suffered, all we had endured together and separately, now counted as nothing.

All for nothing.

I don't remember when our sausage was lifted, when it was swaying, when everything was shifting downward, with my body falling on top of those heated steel drums—I only remember the pain of sunlight hitting my eyes.

CHAPTER 24

BAJA PENINSULA, MEXICO

THE DRYING FLOORS were flat concrete surfaces stretching two miles into the distance, fifty feet wide, separated by railroad tracks, little shacks, and dirt roads. A third of the surfaces were covered with spread-out trash delivered days before, waiting to again be turned over and re-exposed to the dry, stiflingly hot Mexican sun. The other strips were hovered over by self-guided cranes shuttling sausages into place, waiting for the morning shift to arrive and continue the process of cleaning up the oceans.

Dislodging themselves from the tram they'd ridden from the facility entrance, Francisco Alvarez and Alfonso Perez stored their backpacks in a small shack and assumed their positions behind the yellow safety lines. When the control tower confirmed that all was ready, Francisco pressed a button on an operations panel. The crane deftly lowered its sausage onto the floor. Alfonso wielded an air hammer to unscrew the bolts and pop off the metal clamp. He stepped quickly to the side as the cylinder's insides spurted onto the concrete.

The crane, with timed precision, expertly lifted the back end of the sausage and moved away, trailing the tube's insides into a long, heaping mound of rotting fish carcasses, a million plastic bottles, and other sordid trash skimmed from some faraway sea and mashed into the tube. The contents slid out easily, riding a thick river of gelatinous goop gushing across the wide floor until it was turned back by curbs at the edge.

As one crane lifted the empty sausage and motored off, another rolled into place thirty yards away, its hooks holding a sausage like the other but with a bright yellow end. Unsealed by Alfonso and upended, it disgorged, among other things, refrigerators, plastic kiddie swimming pools, large blocks of Styrofoam that had once held up floating docks, an old fishing net, and three sealed steel drums.

It had a lesser amount of goop.

A tractor was already spreading out the first mound of trash as Francisco and Alfonso walked through the pile of the second, sorting materials as they did every day, rolling items off to the side to be hauled away. It was dull work but respected, and as they listened to their iPods in their air-cooled hazmat suits, each man worked at his unvarying pace, measured precisely to match the time of their scheduled breaks.

Alfonso was going about his business when he heard Francisco scream. His rake had turned over a body, then another, and then a third.

Horror was their first response. They bent to wipe away the layers of filth and realized these were not corpses—they were people, alive and struggling to breathe. Trained to handle coworkers who collapsed from the heat, the two men rushed the bodies into the nearby shack which had emergency water sprayers and oxygen masks. Alfonso hit the red emergency button, calling an EMT team.

Washing off goop and glop, strings of seaweed, and lumps

of unknown origin, holding oxygen masks to the faces of the three people lying in front of them, Alfonso and Francisco stared down at two men and a woman—hacking, coughing, vomiting, gasping and holding their hands over their eyes, crying out in pain. Clearly, an accident had happened on the ocean cleaning platform, and these people had mistakenly been trapped in the tube. How long had they been there? It must have been days, but how had they survived on so little air? How could they not have choked on the stench?

It would be a while before the answers were known.

CHAPTER 25

I<small>T WAS SO</small> hot in the tube that it took weeks in the burn unit at San Diego General for the three of us to recover. We were also massively dehydrated from more than a week at sea, and our bodies were in shock. We were malnourished from our wildly out-of-balance diet, our eyes had to be brought slowly back into light to minimize the risk of permanently damaging the retinas, and our skin, exposed to the high levels of toxic sludge we had lived in, required medical wrapping that made each of us look like King Tut's mummy.

I could go on, but understand that our recovery was not a quick process, and even as they addressed the obvious problems, the doctors worried a lot about infections caused by our petri dish of a survival pod. Be assured that we all survived, but the details weren't simple.

The EMTs in Mexico rushed us to the facility's hospital, plugged us into IVs for hydration, and hardly cleaned us up at all because of the danger of pulling off damaged skin. There was no time to fill out paperwork. We were sedated and helicoptered to San Diego, and remained unknown to our doctors for almost a week. None of us had any ID.

Thankfully, in investigating the accident, the Baja facility's security people went through the piles of junk and separated out everything that seemed not to be trash, which included sundry clothing, the diving equipment, our mesh bags, our helmets, respirators, and wetsuits, the unused water bottles, plus five flashlights and an unusual number of unused batteries scattered throughout the rubble.

Most important, going through our clothes produced my cell phone. After carefully charging it, the security people found a picture of me standing next to the richest man in the world, who looked suspiciously like King Tut number three, and that's when the rockets went off. Our presence in the tube was no accident, but they could not conceive why three people would do such a thing.

Thankfully and to their credit, the burn unit doctors at San Diego General steadfastly refused to turn over their famous patient until he'd finished the treatment protocol, which was, fortunately for me, after I was awake, coherent, and talking. When I told the police the body-dumping story and explained to them the cell phone pictures from the freezers, even my own editor was part of the large crowd of news people standing around the front door of the hospital, demanding an interview.

It was a blockbuster news day for the world.

The operations of Parker's ocean cleaning facility were halted and the ship searched by the Coast Guard, which also located, stopped, and searched the ghost-in-the-night freighter and scoured its warehouse on the San Francisco docks.

The results, however, were not what I'd expected. The three people working in the body processing rooms of Parker's cruise ship were of minimal help: they had never seen any of the bodies inside the bags they handled. When the Coast Guard inspected the storage room containers, not a single body was found in any of the containers that wasn't confirmed by paperwork as having been legally obtained from a mortuary, morgue, or coroner's office. It was the same with the freighter and its warehouse. The trucking company, when questioned, claimed absolute innocence as to what was in the bags and produced paperwork that perfectly tracked their business end-to-end—all was as would be expected. The body donors—the morgues and other institutions—confirmed that they had been using Parker's free unclaimed body disposal processes for some time without any problems. Their paperwork, even down to the barcode numbers, was as clean as a whistle.

It was slightly comical to me, but to the rest of the nation, it looked like the big guy rescued from the trash in Mexico was crazy and was out to sully the reputation of the famous Parker Evans. He had obviously photoshopped the pictures on his phone.

I watched the developing stories on my TV in the hospital room, in awe of how efficient Parker's organization was. He must have had meticulous contingency plans that immediately launched an army of people to scrub every trace of his murderous activities. It had to be Van Thiem orchestrating the coverup; I should have stuck the knife in his neck when I had the chance. He was nowhere to be found when the Coast Guard got to the ship, but I had no doubt he was fully in charge of covering his and Parker's tracks.

Everything was looking bad for my version of the body dumping business until the Houston Police Department received a casual complaint from one of its marginal citizens named Evil Ed Nasty, who'd legally changed his name from Edward Kowalowitz to hide the fact that his grandparents were Jewish. Evil Ed was a member of a local biker gang and had lodged a complaint with police that he'd been the victim of fraud. It seems he had answered an online ad that promised money for services rendered, which he admitted to rendering, but then the app on his phone stopped working before he was paid. He didn't really know what a bitcoin was, but he wanted it anyway.

The initial police reaction was to relegate Ed's case to the bottom of their files, but when he staunchly refused to say what service he had rendered, they became suspicious. Leaning on him a bit—in fact, threatening to link him to some other recent biker-related cases—they convinced the Evil one to give up more details about his actions. He'd delivered a package to a certain location, he said, and was due his payment. But suspicion only increased over his claim when he didn't know what was in the package and had no receipt— though he didn't think it should matter to them anyway.

After an hour or so of more pressure, Evil Ed finally told them he'd delivered a bag with a body in it. He assumed it was all part of a legitimate business. No, he had no idea how that body came to be in the bag—he was just a delivery boy. Slowly figuring out that his fraud complaint had been a major mistake, Ed tried to weasel his way out by withdrawing it. Too late. The police were now really intrigued. After a few more hours convinced Ed he might be looking at some serious time, Evil Ed broke down and not only revealed his role in an online murder scheme but also spilled the beans about some of his friends in the same line of work.

The State of Texas kicked into high gear following up his leads. Police immediately tracked down one of the *body-in-a-bag* pickup points and found a warehouse with a few freezers Van Thiem's cleanup army had missed.

That did it. Lots of homeless-looking bodies with bullet holes, knife wounds, and bashed-in heads, all in bags with barcodes similar to those in my pictures. My photos were now assumed to be true, and one of the homeless bodies featured was even matched to a name.

I rooted for all the law enforcement agencies who were in

the hunt, and didn't really mind the onslaught of news people who'd made it their goal to hang Parker Evans from a telephone pole, but I did grow tired of it.

Besides, it no longer mattered. The harsh punishment for Parker I had looked forward to had been superseded by reality. The Parker Evans who went into the tube was not the Parker Evans who came out of it.

Call it mental derangement, call it personality loss, call it madness, call it whatever you want, Parker came out of his burn treatment in an almost-catatonic calm. He talked gibberish when spoken to, looked around the room without interest, and ignored the television. He ate, slept, pooped, and did other things associated with a biological creature, but the man the world had worshipped for so long was no longer in the house.

I think it was the heat in the tube from our day in Mexico that pushed him over the edge, although Molly and I both think he already was irretrievably close. We watched his mental awareness progressively deteriorate during our time on the collection ship, but it wasn't something we were qualified to evaluate, or could do anything about. To be honest, we didn't pay him much attention other than watching to make sure he didn't make our lives worse; we were too busy keeping ourselves alive.

This produced an interesting situation. All of America wanted another O. J. Simpson circus: the normal Parker Evans, exceedingly smart and exceedingly rich but now revealed as a monster of evil, would have dominated media screens for months while a flurry of lawyers battled over particular interpretations of his guilt or innocence. The corporation he had built would have swirled endlessly around him, protecting or persecuting him, depending on who might be construed as an accomplice, while America cheered both ways.

It would have been a true American drama providing the highest quality entertainment, and the ratings would have shot through the roof.

The opposite happened.

Since finding him mentally incompetent was not a close call, Parker could not be charged with any crimes and could not go to trial. This worked out well for the company, whose board of directors worked quickly to dump all the responsibility, guilt, and—most importantly—all the liability on poor Parker's immensely talented head, declaring he had done it without their knowledge. They all walked away.

America was vastly disappointed. The rich guy had gotten away with murder. Public opinion held that going crazy was the least he deserved, and then turned its attention to seeking some other public figure who could give them the higher level of the drama the nation relished. The viewing public relegated Parker to the status of a living nonentity, a non-contributor to society, a person who could only take and not give, which reminded me very much of those homeless people he had sent to the bottom of the ocean.

He had become his own victim.

CHAPTER 26

ALTHOUGH MOLLY and I left like any other discharged patient, a nurse told us that Parker had been taken out at night, escorted by a contingent of doctors, lawyers, and security guards. From what I understand, he was taken to some obscure psychiatric hospital outside Boston and placed under the supervision of a world-renowned psychiatrist who just happened to be on Parker's board of directors.

The doctor requested privacy for the family, even though Parker had none, and the corporation restarted the ocean cleaning platform the next day. Nothing was ever said about resuming the legitimate side of the body-dumping business.

Once we passed through the hospital's front door, Molly and I were mobbed by reporters, photographers, and onlookers, and were immediately scheduled for a solid month of radio and TV talk shows and national news interviews. By the end of the first week, I had a book contract with Random House that gave me $1 million upfront in addition to royalties. They wanted a hard-hitting, blow-by-blow retelling of a genius gone crazy while under the guise of saving the world. Meanwhile, Molly used her new-found fame to sign up with an Antarctic research ship as the next year's summer intern. She had always wanted to see penguins.

We both made it on *Good Morning America*.

As the month went on, life slowed down. Parker's dealings with dead bodies became old news, and calls for justice were stymied by his now widely known and legally confirmed madness. It pretty seriously limited the enjoyment of watching Parker's future unfold, and the public slowly lost interest.

Molly and I also lost interest in being recognized in the street, and after our fifteen minutes of fame was repeated several times, we both returned home, looking forward to getting on with life. But saying goodbye after our last interview was tough. We were no longer fellow combatants, but the bonds we felt inside still were strong, and we could only marvel at the depths of a friendship forged in the darkness of hell.

I was happy to be home, though, and felt a whole new dimension of appreciation for my family. I was again with people who were honest and excited and truthful and relaxed and who shared my values. I reveled in not having to worry about deceit, pretense, or hidden purposes.

Beth and I were better friends, anxious to talk to each other, touching, holding hands, lying in bed and learning anew how to caress each other with tenderness. My kids called on a regular basis, I learned to use the *see-them-while-speaking-to-them* app on my phone when my grandkids wanted to talk, and everything seemed clean and fresh.

I wish it had lasted.

The next week, I had a nightmare that had me up and pacing in the middle of the night, waiting for my heart to stop racing. I figured I was just coming down from the high of our survival, the publicity and fleeting fame, my medication, and the enhanced appreciation for a physical life full of people, light, water, food, and clean air.

I called Molly, wondering if she had had any anxiety problems, but she said she was fine. She admitted being embarrassed by occasional uncontrollable rants to her friends about Parker's evils, but she was sleeping as well as ever.

I returned to work, breathing the freshest of air, drinking the clearest of water, maybe a gallon a day, and enjoying the brightness of the sky. Instead of the planned article about Parker's ocean cleaning platform, the paper ran two first-person stories describing my time on the ship and the escape from Parker's clutches. But I couldn't include everything—my contract with Random House made me hold back enough to make sure their book would still be fresh and absorbing, a blockbuster that would be worth their money.

When the articles hit the newsstands, Molly and I did another round of interviews. We talked freely about our journey, but if interviewers asked about details of our time in the prison tube, we both brushed over them lightly and used humor to sidestep the horrors we were hoping to forget. After the initial articles and interviews and hype, my nights returned to normal, but when the second rush of publicity brought more remembering, it meant more dreams of darkness and despair came with them.

At first, there were common patterns: being trapped in a coffin-like enclosure, feeling wrapped up tight and immobile like a mummy, being shrouded in darkness and unable to open my eyes despite all my efforts, and yelling to someone who could never hear me. In other dreams, I had an intense need for food, I was suffocating in clouds of stench, floating in an endless sea whose waves constantly drenched me, knocked me down, and rolled me over, and I was abandoned on a remote planet, alone, with no possibility of rescue.

I even had a dream where there was an overwhelming stink of pee in the air.

I understood and was patient with myself, as was Beth. Trauma does this, and my agonies were like the PTSD that affects soldiers in war as well as others who are psychically maimed. I had had a scare, that's all—a deeply personal, deeply intense, deeply terrifying scare that had scrambled my brain for a while. Given time, I would heal.

But I did not.

My nightly hauntings worsened—screaming, weeping, and sorrow deep enough to shake me uncontrollably, followed by wave upon wave of bare-naked guilt, though for what, I could never be sure.

I talked it over with Beth, and it seemed best that I move to the guest bedroom. I didn't want to and kept hoping some kind of bond would keep me from doing it, but she was growing as exhausted from my nightly outbursts as I was. It worked, at least for her, and the house was a better place to live. For myself, I was now alone in the darkness, and it increased my dread of what the night would bring. I took more sleeping pills, which helped some, and cut my hours at the paper so I could sleep later if I needed to. But despite any little improvements, I felt I was dropping further into a despair I didn't understand and could do nothing about.

My nightly visits by demons continued. Two months passed. The terrible thoughts I'd assumed would be transient had made themselves at home. I had not settled down, I had not healed, and I grew afraid I was following the path I'd seen in Parker—the path to permanent, crippling, overwhelming madness. If that was true, I no longer wanted to live.

———

I TOOK to visiting Starbucks early each morning, buying a large coffee and a donut, and then sitting and watching people come and go, thinking about their busy little ordinary lives and wondering if I would ever be ordinary again. On my way one morning, I was stopped at a light when there was a tapping on the window. It was Jimmy A. He handed me a torn piece of paper with an address on it.

"Thought you might like to visit this place," he said. "Purty interesting."

The light changed, he stepped back, and I drove on. I hadn't even worked in a decent hello.

In a Walmart parking lot, I typed the address into my navigation system. I didn't know what to expect. I hadn't thought about Jimmy and the others for more than half a year. They and their stories had slipped to the back of my mind and then vanished altogether.

Or so I thought. It took more than half an hour to wind my way through the backstreets of downtown.

"You did the newspaper articles about the homeless. We were told you might come by. I'm Jerrod Harrison, the resident aide."

I acknowledged what I'd written and shook his hand.

The building Jimmy had sent me to was nondescript, to be complimentary. It was old, three stories, and might have once been an apartment house, or maybe a school or office building. Anything on the outside identifying it had long since disappeared.

It was now a worn-out dump.

Jerrod, however, seemed bright and interesting enough, and offered to show me around.

It was home to a variety of men—most of them alcoholics who now drink little, or homeless wanderers too worn out to beg anymore, or men with brains dulled down to minimal functioning.

"Our residents don't really have any classifications," Jerrod said. "When they land here, everyone is pretty much the same. We're kind of the last step in our residents' lives. Technically, we offer low-cost housing to non-dependent alcoholics, but we accept anyone who doesn't have another place to go. We're not social workers, per se," he said, although he confessed to having the certification, "but it's the worker part we don't do; we provide the social part. We charge $10 a day for a place to sleep, coffee and donuts for breakfast, a sandwich and punch for lunch, and soups for an evening meal, with vegetables. We always have cookies and coffee available."

"I don't remember ever hearing of this place."

"That's pretty much on purpose. We ask you don't mention it either."

I understood his request much better as we toured the building. There was a kitchen and dining room on the first floor created by knocking down walls between apartments. Similar rooms held old sofas, easy chairs, and round tables for playing cards or putting together puzzles. A single large room had been created out of several apartments on each floor.

"We represent an association of similarly minded people," the young man said. "It's not quite a nonprofit group because there's no central organization and no formal IRS designation, plus our donors would rather not be publicly associated with our work."

It had been an apartment building, he said, but the large rooms now held rows of sleeping cubicles about five feet wide by eight feet long by seven feet high. The walls were plywood screwed together at the corners, with a ceiling of stretched chicken wire that let air circulate while still giving a feeling of individual security. Each cheap plywood door had a padlock whose key was kept at the desk like an old-time hotel. There was a latch on the inside.

My host opened an unoccupied cubicle. It had a single bed

frame with a mattress, sheets, a blanket, a pillow, a built-in shelf screwed to the wall, and a small rug.

"Realistically," Jerrod said, lowering his voice, "we're one step above a piece of cardboard on the sidewalk, although we do wash the sheets on a regular basis."

I counted and guessed that if the third floor was like the second, the building might have a maximum of sixty or seventy residents. A number of original bathrooms offered a sink, toilet, and tub for every six to ten cubicles—if the bathrooms worked.

When I was growing up, my dad called places like this *flophouses*. You didn't rent a room, you rented a place to lie down. In my dad's hometown's early days, when there were several times more people than rooms, hotel owners would use chalk to mark rectangles on the floor where patrons could sleep. Forget about a mattress, and the blankets were a penny apiece.

"Sometimes a resident will stay an inappropriate amount of time in the bathroom and the others will pee in a corner," the man said. "We provide reusable plastic jugs for them, but some people wait until it's too late, or have bad aim. In extreme cases, we have toilet seats on top of buckets and plastic bags, but that's if someone is taking a diuretic or has a bowel disorder."

We walked through the third floor, then went down to the lobby and sat at a small table in the one true apartment, reserved for the resident aide.

After all my interviews with the destitute and seeing the range of emotions connected to homelessness and poverty, I still was horrified to see the conditions these men lived in. It was a stained, musty, small, self-imposed semi-prison defined mostly by the smell of urine, peeling paint, and threadbare carpets. I had no problem imagining rats, mice, and cockroaches as daily companions.

But I understood.

If the city health department ever found this place, if the fire marshal ever made a visit, if a building inspector ever walked through the doors, even if nearby residents ever crossed the threshold, this building would be closed in a heartbeat. If that happened, the men living here and laying their heads on the long-used mattresses would have no place to go except for far-less-adequate shelters and bottom-of-the-barrel housing basements, or into the streets. If abandoned, most of them would quickly die. Alone.

"Uh, how many people end up dying here?" I asked.

The young man gave a thoughtful look, then answered without hesitation. "It varies from year to year, with more dying typically in the winter since the holidays bring more depression, but I'd guess that about a quarter of our residents pass away in a typical year. Some of them will have come recently, while others have been here for some time. Some family members will move a dying man to a hospice because it's something insurance will pay for, so we don't count those. Some residents drift away or go back home, and we never know what happens with them. So overall, it varies, but it's something we never get comfortable with. It's always a hard day when you have to break into a cubicle because someone's not responding."

I understood what he was implying. This was where lonely men at the very end of life came to die, their last stop before the morgue. The benefit here is that someone will notice. And it's better than an alley.

"How do you manage expenses?" I asked.

"The breads and pastries are day-old and donated by a bakery, the coffee comes from a truck stop, the soups are made with free ingredients from a local farm co-op, the operating funds come from a few individuals, and any cash donations we get go to utilities and upkeep."

"How do the residents find out to come here?"

"The original social media—people talk to each other. Believe it or not, our residents want to be here."

"What's the average age?"

"I'm not sure because we don't ask, but I'd guess that most of them are between sixty and seventy. There are a few older, hardly any younger. Most are alcoholics but rarely drink to excess because they can't afford it. We make no judgments and set no restrictions. Being relatively old and feeble pretty much keeps them from being overly violent or even resistant. Most sleep a lot. We don't accept those with obvious mental illness because we can't provide what they need.

"We provide a sense of community," Jerrod said quietly but with conviction. "Most of our society wants nothing to do with this level of humanity, but our residents look a lot the same, so they do well at accepting and tolerating each other. There's a certain measure of grace among them, and no one holds anyone more guilty than they hold themselves. You might even be proud of how they treat each other."

He looked at me with sadness but conviction. "For these people, it's a hell of a lot better than being alone."

Medical problems?

"We have a couple of doctors and two nurses who offer us their time on a part-time basis. That gets most patients an adequate balance of medicines they need and painkillers. We don't have a bus or van or even a car to take people to treatment centers or the hospital.

"We don't have that level of resources. To be blunt, though, most of our residents don't want treatments if they can take care of their pains with over-the-counter drugs. If they don't already know what's killing them, they don't want to find out. They won't go for MRIs or x-rays or exams or to be tested for serious diseases. There's more fear of treatment than there is of sickness, and if they can just get their pain managed, they're okay with that."

Does anyone have family?

"It's not easy to believe when you look around, but most of the men here are paying customers. Almost all of them have some kind of Social Security or retirement or qualify for Medicaid. Usually, the money goes to some designated family member, who we ask to pay the daily rate. Mostly it lets us hire custodians, because the conditions can sometimes be pretty bad and volunteers often aren't able to handle the sadness."

Any city, state or federal funding?

"I wish," the man said, "but we'd never be approved. We wouldn't make it past the most basic provisions to qualify for funding, so we don't even fill out the paperwork. Think of us as a niche business that stays below the radar of any officials in a position to help us."

His eyes met mine. "I wouldn't be truthful if I said that what we do here is a ministry or a treatment facility or a halfway house, or anything positive. It's not. Our residents have no other place to go, so we offer mercy, not hope."

I was getting too close to a confessional. I had only one more question.

"What do they need most?"

The man thought a moment, and his answer was clear: "Our residents need compassion. They need to know that they're not alone, and that they are worthy human beings. There's not a person here who thinks he's getting anything other than what he earned in life, and most of them have come to peace with it. Even if they hurt down to their bones, or are lonely, or feel abandoned, each one of them appreciates that this place exists and that we welcome them. Our residents need a smile and a friendly handshake when they come through the door. They know they're not likely to walk out."

CHAPTER 27

"I WANT to go see Parker, and I want you to go with me."

There was a stunned silence on the other end of the line. "Are you nuts? What in the world for?"

I had been on the phone with Molly for several minutes. She was now having frightening dreams. Talking to friends helped, but the dreams had gotten worse, and she found herself jerking awake at night, unable to let them go. We'd exchanged emails, but this was the first time I'd heard her voice in a while.

Having made my pitch and gotten her question in return, it was my turn to be silent. I couldn't give a good reason. "Look," I finally said, "I really don't know why. Maybe it's to see if he's any better, maybe it's even wanting to see somebody who I can pity more than me. I feel like I'm going crazy, and I'll try anything to keep it from happening."

"You know I don't give a rat's ass about the guy, right? I'd still kick him if he got close."

"I understand. But what are you doing about your dreams?"

There was another silence. "Nothing really, I guess," she said slowly. "I assume they'll go away."

"I've been thinking that for two months, and it hasn't worked. I think seeing Parker will help. I think both of us seeing Parker will help."

"You know, I'm pretty tired right now. Losing my nights is a bitch."

"You can sleep on the plane. We need to go now."

"I thought you were feeling old. Aren't you the guy who complained so much about feeling old?"

"I lied. It was just a ruse to make sure you didn't fall in love with a big, strong guy like me. Listen, you can make your own decision, but I really need to see Parker."

"Do you even know where he is?"

"Hey, I'm an investigative reporter. I'll find out."

————

THE EVERGREENS IS a psychiatric hospital disguised as a celebrity resort. Whenever you hear of some movie star or politician or musician going to rehab, The Evergreens is likely to be the place. They have a staff of experienced doctors, a beautiful facility with swimming pools, saunas, spas, tennis courts, jogging trails, and gourmet restaurants, plus a security system as good as Fort Knox.

My first impression of The Evergreens' CEO, Dr. Wilson Moore, was that of an obese politician. The resume and history I'd read online were impressive, but I had trouble getting past his triple crown as a member of Parker's board of directors, his legal guardian, and his psychiatrist. Conflict of interest would be a mild description of the situation.

My prejudices increased after Molly and I visited his office —it was twice the size of Parker's cabin on the cruise ship, with walls full of pictures of him and several past presidents, governors, heads of state, and foreign dignitaries. He'd once been a genuine working psychiatrist with an actual practice but had realized his true calling was establishing a niche treatment facility that could rake in untold amounts of money from famous people who needed private treatments for their various ills. He's now a public figurehead who spends his days playing golf with his cronies.

Did I say I didn't like him?

"Dr. Evans will never recover," Moore said matter-of-factly. "He hasn't responded to treatment, hasn't progressed on any of the tests we've given him, if he agrees to take them at all, and does nothing but wander blindly about his rooms. It's a clear case of accelerated decline in mental capacity compounded by severe personality abandonment."

Sounded like a clear case of accelerated bullshit to me.

Because we had been Parker's companions in suffering and were famous enough there'd be bad publicity if we were refused a friendly visit, Moore led Molly and me along a series of walking paths surrounded by immense beds of flowers, ferns, bushes, ponds, finely cut grass, and tall picturesque trees. We passed a number of cottages where I assumed patients stayed, and finally came to a remote larger house in the back of the complex. It was of proper Craftsman style, with a rambling wooden porch hidden under a large roof held up by a series of carefully shingled wooden pillars.

Stately growths of ivy covered one side of the cottage and climbed solidly up the chimney, while large oak trees shaded the side yards. We were escorted up the porch steps and through a thick front door of polished oak, noticing only as it was shut that steel reinforcing bars had been grafted into the back. It was a very artfully made prison door.

For all the architectural comfort expressed by the house's exterior, the inside was unremarkable, with only two over-stuffed chairs and a sofa around a fireplace in the front room and a modern metal table-and-chair set in the kitchen. There were no shelves, no books, no pictures, no drapes, no rugs, no decorations.

Moore introduced us to the nurses—I counted three—as we walked down a hallway into Parker's suite—bedroom, bathroom, and sitting room. The decor seriously clashed with the rest of the house. The beautifully polished wooden floors had been covered with harsh white linoleum, the bare walls were white, and fluorescent bulbs in industrial-sized fixtures hung from the ceiling. The look was sterile, to say the least.

The bedroom had a typical multi-positional hospital bed with white sheets, a metal wheeled stand with IV bag hangers and electronic monitors, an armoire-type closet, little white storage shelves near the bed, a TV on the wall, and a plush recliner as the only comfortable-looking piece of furniture. The room gave the impression of being antiseptically clean, neat, and well-kept for the ultimate in-patient care—until you noticed the belt-like arm and leg restraints attached to the bed.

Another nurse, Margaret Steele, according to her nametag, joined our entourage. Apparently, she was the head nurse, so that made four nurses dedicated to Parker and his little cottage. I wondered if Parker might have reverted to being violent or something. Remembering how much he squirmed while he was taped up, I could well imagine he might be difficult to handle in other situations.

Parker Evans, my grown-up friend from elementary school who I had played with at recess and after school, stood alone across the room without acknowledging we had walked in the door. He just kept looking out the window.

Molly and I walked across the room and stood next to him, trying to get his attention, but he continued to seem oblivious to our presence.

Parker did not look well. As opposed to the healthy, fit man I had met on his cruise ship, he was now haggard and unshaved, with long, unkempt hair that was surprisingly gray. It hadn't occurred to me that he dyed his hair. He had lost his tan, his robust frame, and looked surprisingly frail.

What was most remarkable was his clothes. He looked like a bum, with stains on his misbuttoned shirt, the zipper open on his pants, and a mishmash of creases front and back on both. He looked downright shabby and smelled as if he had peed on himself.

"He refuses to change clothes," Steele explained. "We forced him into new clothes one day, and he just pulled them off, threw them on the floor, and walked around naked. He refused to dress at all until we brought his old clothes back."

"I told them to let him be," Dr. Moore half-apologized. "We shouldn't force him to do anything that really isn't important. If he wishes to appear any particular way, then it's his choice. Likewise, with his beard. He'd never worn one as long as I've known him, but he refuses for us to modify his appearance in any way."

We were both stunned. I would have understood if we had found a vegetable, but that implies someone who has no will or ability to do anything by choice. It was not the case here. Parker was exerting his will and making choices, bad though they were perceived, which made me question exactly how damaged he was.

Could he be pretending?

And what was this idea of *making choices* anyway? Moore had described Parker's condition in part as *personality abandonment*. Forcing the staff to obey his clothing choices didn't sound as if he had abandoned anything.

Molly suddenly kicked his ankle and screamed, "Move your feet, asshole!"

If I was startled, the doctor and nurse almost fell over.

But Parker turned, looked at her, and smirked.

There! I'd seen that smirk before. In the light of a flashlight, any touching of their feet in the crowded net had been grounds for verbal combat. I thought it became something they each relished. There was no question that Parker Evans still lived in the body before us. Perhaps damaged, perhaps broken, perhaps only partly connected to reality, but something of him remained.

He lost the smirk, his eyes turned back to the window, and his face returned to looking null and void.

"She hasn't changed a bit, has she?" I said with a smile, hoping for a response. I got none—he continued to stare ahead as if I wasn't there.

"He won't answer," Moore said, having regained his composure. "I believe his connections to reality have all been severed. We're purely in the mode of preventing him from hurting himself."

Was that the treatment the doctor had referred to? Prevention? I wanted to ask more, but it would have done no good and would have made me more disgusted than I already was. This whole place was just a fancy prison to keep Parker from ever again interacting with the world.

Perhaps he couldn't. Perhaps he shouldn't. What's the punishment for causing thousands of people to be murdered?

I motioned to Molly, and she followed me as I turned and sat on the side of his hospital bed.

"Does he have dreams?" I asked. "Does he wake up at night frightened or screaming?"

The doctor and the nurse were taken aback. "Oh, well, no," the nurse said. "Not at all. We give him a sedative every night. When he first came, he never slept except for short naps. He'd get out of bed and stand at the window."

"Not sleeping isn't healthy behavior," Moore said. "He needs his sleep or else he'll never cooperate."

"Does he ever talk to himself?" Molly asked. "Has he ever lectured you on polymer science?"

Again, it was as if they'd never heard of such a thing.

This wasn't turning out to be what I expected, and it was ruining any sort of closure I had hoped for. Had they given Parker a chance to recover? Were they planning on him recovering? Were they trying to keep him from recovering? Is Dr. Jerk only concerned with keeping him manageable and silent for the rest of his life?

I was ready to leave until I thought of something. "Do you know where there might be a marine salvage yard in Boston?" I asked. "Or maybe a nautical antique store?"

I'm pretty sure Moore was about to reserve me a room down the hall because of the clear disconnect he saw in my brain. Even Molly looked at me in wonder. Steele suggested going to the wharf and looking around, or maybe Googling for a location. It was Boston—you'd expect all sorts of marine stuff.

"Do you mind if I bring a gift back for Parker?" I asked. "Just something from his old friends? It won't be anything dangerous, I promise. I need to run into town to get it, but I think he might perk right up when he sees it."

Moore obviously didn't like the idea, but I kept reframing the benefit of gift-giving until he came around. Maybe he remembered I was an official member of the media.

"We'll be back after lunch," I told them.

———

"WHAT THE HELL IS THIS?"

Dr. Moore was not happy. He had come back to the office in an upbeat mood after his noon golf game and the usual nineteenth hole's worth of drinks with his fellow rich guys. But he found an urgent message from Nurse Steele at Parker's cottage, and he went right over.

"What the hell is this?" he asked again.

The mattress and pillows had been pulled off the bed and slung on the floor at its foot, the sheet rudely pulled back. The recliner had been extended and then laid on its side, leaning on the edge of the mattress. One of the small tables was upended and its drawer pulled out.

Over it all, draped from one side to the other and folded so that it made a floor on the mattress and a top above it, was a portion of an old fishing net, complete with floats, crumpled, dirty, and loosely hung.

In it, snuggled up inside the nest the net had made, holding firmly onto the twine of the weave, snoring softly as he cradled a beaming flashlight, was Parker Evans, probably having his best sleep in a long time.

———

"THAT WAS the dumbest thing I've ever done."

"No, it wasn't. It was the most compassionate thing you've ever done. Compassion is everything."

Molly and I were sitting in the airport terminal, waiting for her flight to board. We had sat and talked and laughed and felt more together than in a long time. It covered up the increased pity we now had for Parker Evans, two-time Nobel Prize recipient and the King of Trash.

"You know they'll just throw it all out and put the room back the way it was," she said.

I nodded. It had been a fool's quest. There was no way to rescue Parker from an entrenched establishment filthy with money and consumed by the fear of losing it, so my little theatrics was solely a personal gesture for someone who used to be my friend. I knew I was right about Dr. Moore and his treatment: Parker was not at The Evergreens to get better but to be kept confined. His mind was probably truthfully and permanently broken. There was no treatment that could make him a functioning human being again, a participant in regular society, but I couldn't help wanting him to at least have a good sleep.

Our attempt at giving the finger to Dr. Jerk and his staff was small and fleeting, but maybe Parker—if he had just one more encounter with what the three of us had shared for all those dark, lonely times—might find something remaining inside himself that would let him do more than just stare out the window.

"Here, this is for you," Molly said as her flight was called. She handed me a paper sack.

I looked askance at it, opened it, and laughed. Inside was a wadded-up piece of the fishing net, with a token float attached, and a flashlight.

"It's a survival kit," she said. "Remember all the rules we made to keep ourselves sane? They still apply. I made me one, too. I'm going to put it on my nightstand, and I'm going to lay everything out every night before I go to bed. When I have a nightmare, I'm going to grab hold of the net and turn on my flashlight. I'm hoping it will tell me that everything is going to be okay. You ought to try it, too."

It was no wonder I had been dazzled by this fine woman.

"And I'm going to remember straddling you in that hot tub," she whispered with a wink. "You're obviously not as old as you think you are."

She pressed tight against me, pulled my head down, kissed my lips, and was gone.

CHAPTER 28

THERE ARE a couple of episodes of a TV drama where a main character is shot by a bad guy and barely survives the subsequent surgery and recovery. After he's released, he has flashbacks and panic attacks and is forced to visit a trauma specialist. He makes the visit, recounts the days before and after the shooting, and is helped to recognize what had happened, what was continuing to happen, and what would allow him to move on.

The day of the shooting, the character had attended a performance of a musical group that performed several songs. After the shooting and his recovery, every time he heard a similar musical group, his brain reacted by taking him back to the horror of the night he was shot, which brought on the panic attacks. Once the trauma specialist identifies and explains the connection, the character stops having flashbacks and panic attacks.

I had hoped that if Molly and I visited Parker, maybe the three of us being together again would bring closure to this scary episode of my life and it would stop my episodes of spiraling depression.

It didn't work the way I thought it would.

Laying waste to my vast knowledge of human behavior gleaned from the depths of media programming, it was Molly's gift to me that provided my salvation. I did, indeed, set the old net and flashlight on my nightstand, grabbing them and holding them close whenever I woke up in a panic. I would remember the closing and sealing of the tube, the immense suffering while inside, and then, most importantly, the day Molly and I walked out of the hospital into the bright Mexican sunshine. Repeating that memory as I physically held the fishing net and glowing flashlight, brought out a deep compassion for myself as I re-experienced the beginning and the end of my trauma. It provided the intimate comfort I needed to combat the depression by returning to me the feeling of having a nest that could not be taken away.

I wept a heartfelt thanks when my nightmares decreased to bad dreams and then to ordinary dreams and then disappeared altogether. My screaming fits and periods of weeping became short periods of thoughtfulness and reflection. Once it seemed that the changes were here to stay, Beth invited me back into the bedroom, and I wasted no time in accepting.

Dorothy in the Wizard of Oz said that there's no place like home, but she had yet to know the sweet embrace of the one you love.

Molly experienced a similar rescue from her nightmares, and we couldn't help but be amazed at the wonders that were our bodies and minds. Molly's sacks brought the strangest, most disturbing, and most violent experiences of our lives to a close.

Now all I had to do was write a book about it.

———

I EXPECTED it to be pretty straightforward. Having been through multiple interviews in which I was quizzed about every facet of our experience, I had the details on instant recall. Parker's and my early life together as friends, since there was so little of it, wasn't hard to remember. What happened in between had been covered by a half-dozen Parker Evan biographies, hundreds of his interviews, and a few thousand other sources, including some nasty articles in the supermarket rags.

I was ready to write the book, or at least thought I was. Random House worked with me on the publisher's expectations and schedules. Rather than grinding out a basic tell-all biography, we decided to make it a more focused story centered on Parker's work in the international community that had caused his world view to evolve and eventually become flawed when his passion got ahead of his values. The meat of the book would be a blow-by-blow account of his and my encounter, conflict, attempted resolution, and then the gory details of the tube adventure and subsequent change of life. My difficulties adjusting to the normal world would be included, and the editors were salivating when I told them of the visit to Parker's cottage and Molly's gift.

From my point of view, the new approach made the book easier to write and certainly more interesting than a hefty biography would be, so I plunged ahead with a full head of steam until something happened that stopped me cold.

CHAPTER 29

"You can't write? Well, if you can't write your stories, I'll be stuck with the comics and the political cartoons. Ain't nobody else worth reading in the whole newspaper."

I would have laughed, but my mood was too grim. I had been shut inside my room at home for a week, struggling to write. It was taking far more energy than it should have while producing few words that sounded authentic or gave the right tone to my emotions. Everything I wrote looked jumbled, anxious, and high schoolish. I felt lost and bewildered.

"I'll buy you a *National Enquirer*. You can keep up with the alien sightings."

Jimmy A guffawed at the thought.

Don't ask me why I chose to talk with him after I had written and deleted, written and deleted umpteen times before I faced the reality that I was stuck at a dead end. With disgust and a large amount of embarrassment, I turned my computer off and fled. I had to talk to someone, to get it out, to understand what was going on, and hopefully get myself going again.

I had finished my daily sit-and-stare at Starbucks and was driving home when I saw Jimmy walking along the street. I pulled over, beeped, and we drove to a parking lot where we now sat under a streetlight.

"So, not being able to write has given you the willies, being that you're a professional and all."

"Yeah. Big time. I can't remember a time when I couldn't even write a decent sentence. I don't know how to get myself out of this, and I'm flat-out spooked."

Jimmy was smoking his cigarillo as usual, entertaining himself by repeatedly blowing a thin, accurate stream of smoke into the air.

"Maybe it was being shut up in the dark for a week."

I was surprised. "I didn't expect you to have kept up with my latest adventures."

"Adventures? Damned visit to hell, if you ask me. Scared the pee out of me when I read about it, so I can't imagine what it must have felt like for you."

Scared the pee out of me, too. I had wondered over and over if maybe the closure I thought I'd found wasn't real, and that my current problem was just another result of my terrors at the hands of Parker and Company. But I didn't think so—it felt too ordinary to not be real.

Jimmy turned and looked at me. "Maybe you're still scared. Sometimes, when I get all nervous and ticky and shaky and such, it's just damn fear that's crept up on me when I wasn't looking."

If he wanted to know about being scared, I was going to tell him some of my dreams, then thought better of it. I really just wanted a peaceable conversation that might help me straighten myself out. Besides, he probably had some pretty severe tales of growing up black in America, and I didn't want to start a competition.

"Well, I will admit a lot of things I could be scared about, but it doesn't feel like fear. It's more confusing than that. I worked through the stuff about Parker's work with the UN and different international scientific communities, and it went okay. He was definitely a mover and a shaker. That got me to what happened on the ship. When I tried writing the intense stuff about confronting Parker with his bad ways, the words just stopped, and I couldn't go forward.

"I wanted to be absolutely honest about what was said, but the ground fell out from under me and I ended up feeling lost, like the story was refusing to be told. I'm stuck."

"What do they call it when a writer is all stoved up and can't seem to do anything?" he asked.

"You're probably thinking about writer's block. I know it sounds like it, but I'm in a worse place than that. There's something inside me that's got its fingers around my throat, some kind of hidden force that's strangling me. Do you see anything different about me? Anything that looks like I've changed?"

Jimmy laughed. "You have to remember you're talking to a guy who eats out of dumpsters. Can't expect a lot of insight from the level of life where I operate. But at the risk of sounding cheap, nope, I don't see anything different. Whatever you're dealing with is invisible to the rest of us."

————

JIMMY DIED THE NEXT NIGHT. A drunk driver trying to make a turn through a red light caught the median Jimmy was standing on. The car jumped up and over, taking Jimmy with it. His body would lie around at the morgue for six months, waiting to be claimed. What happened to him after that, I didn't want to know.

I regret never buying him that fresh pack of cigarillos.

CHAPTER 30

TRYING to settle with his being gone, or maybe out of curiosity, or maybe even as yet another excuse to avoid my writing desk, I set out to find Jimmy's house, the sweet place that was his pride and joy. I started with where I saw him the most.

"The traffic is always flowing," he told me once, talking about the intersections near my neighborhood. "There's two malls close to my sweet home and lots of other places to eat and shop down the road. Lots of people who give me a hand are repeats. I see them every day as I'm walking to work. If I work the same spots, people get used to me, and appreciate my wave and my smile, and it makes them more willing to give me money. They not only know I'm poor but they believe it when they see me working."

Between the neighborhoods with private homes and the scattered malls and business districts, it should have been easy to find a fenced-in lot with junk cars behind an industrial-looking building. It wasn't. I spent a lot of time driving up and down streets before I found it a good ten blocks away, which must have taken him a considerable time to walk at the start and end of his day.

Gripping a two-foot piece of PVC in case of any lurking beasts, I squeezed through an opening in the chain-link fence and high-stepped it through the weeds between the rusted cars to the cheap, semi-collapsed storage building, calling out and giving sharp whistles in case a new tenant had already moved in. I heard no reply. I struggled past the bent door into a fairly comfortable place, if you don't mind living on your knees.

A piece of old carpet was draped over a refrigerator box, and a folded blanket was inside on top of a sleeping bag spread out over a thick piece of foam. A half-filled trash bag of crushed aluminum cans sat next to a disorderly stack of magazines, and several hand-written cardboard signs were piled in the corner. Jimmy's empty-and-ready toilet bucket sat near the door. A number of stick-to-anything plastic hooks were on the corrugated walls. I saw two pairs of worn pants hanging on them along with a couple of shirts, a coat-and-rope combination, plus several hats and stocking caps. It was surprisingly neat and tidy.

Negotiating the foam, I crawled into the box and lay down on the sleeping bag, pulling my knees up to fit myself completely inside.

It was cramped, and turning over would have been difficult, but it was cozy and I felt protected and safe. I ignored the smell of the foam, the sleeping bag, and the grime of the blanket. I had smelled worse.

There was enough light coming into the building to see. I propped my head up with a blanket and found myself looking at Jimmy's collection of political buttons. There must have been twenty or twenty-five pinned to the cardboard in a neat row near the top of the box's wall.

One large one had an American flag, and big-name buttons backed Hillary, Trump, Reagan, Bush, Clinton, as well as local candidates.

Support the Democrats, Support the Republicans, Support the Libertarians. I was sure he'd pick a button to match the yard signs in the neighborhood he was working. There were buttons with trees and leaves, one with the silhouette of a dog circled by *American Humane Society*, another with a cat's paw, one urging us to *Save the Whales*, and others with ideological or funny or witty thoughts.

I smiled, remembering how smart Jimmy always seemed at his profession.

In the corner of the display, a plain fifty-cent-sized red button was separate from the others. I couldn't guess what it was for, but it looked familiar.

Then I remembered. I scrunched my head farther into the blanket and stared.

I had been shoved into the overstuffed chair in Parker's cabin suite after waiting for the helicopter that never came. The night before, I had unzipped the body bags in the containers and discovered the murdered bodies of the homeless destined for the conveyor belt that led to the tube that would carry them down to the ocean floor, where they would remain forever.

As I'd squirmed in anger and pain, Parker lectured me on his rationale for consigning the leeches of our society to deep-sea graves. He was so proud of himself, so proud of his solution to an intractable problem, so proud he had had the courage to make a hard decision, and so ashamed of me for being a coward.

He had drawn a circle on a piece of paper he'd put on the end table next to my chair and colored it red, like the button I was staring at. He pointed at the overstuffed chair opposite me.

Imagine a man sitting in that chair over there, one of your homeless buddies, Parker had said. *The man's old, he's sick, he never feels good, he can't stand up straight, he can't even think straight.*

He pees his pants but refuses to wear adult diapers because he thinks they're beneath his dignity. He smells bad. There is no job he can do, even the simplest. He limps in a crooked shuffle, and gasps for air.

But it's up to you to support him. Out of your meager salary, you have to provide him with shelter and food and be kind to him, in spite of the fact that he's robbing your family of time, money, and other resources because you've chosen to make him your responsibility.

Or, Parker said with a smirk, pointing to what he had drawn on the table, *you could press this magic button. Push it, and you get your life back.*

I had made some kind of argument against the existence of such a button, but he grabbed my hand and forced my finger down on the red circle. The old, decrepit, homeless man in Parker's imagination vanished, and the chair became empty. Like that chair, I had been released from my responsibility.

What Parker hadn't known—what he wouldn't have believed—is if he had given me a little more time to think, a little more reflection, a little more staring at the smelly old man he conjured up across from me, he would not have had to force my finger down on his button. I would have pushed it myself.

I stared at the red button pinned to the side of the cardboard box, and I knew the truth. I held my index finger above it, hesitated, aimed my eyes at its redness, and then slowly put my fingertip on top and pressed against it.

The magic worked, and some nameless, homeless man standing on a nameless street corner somewhere vanished.

As tears came to my eyes, I pushed the button again, wanting Sally B to disappear so she wouldn't be a threat, then once more for the other mentally ill homeless I had interviewed. I pushed it again, hoping that my local thug Randy D would not only disappear but also, in some way, roast in hell.

Push the red button and they're all gone, Parker had told me. It was a magic button. No pain, no lingering, no cost, no law-breaking, no condemnation from others, no concerns from friends or relatives, no anything.

There is no guilt. Push the button, and it will be as if someone had never existed.

Hidden from everyone in the world, hidden inside Jimmy's refrigerator box bedroom, I pushed the button because I wanted the world that those people lived in to leave me alone —let me think about other things, let me support other things, let me write about other things, let me care about other things.

I pushed the button for all those people on the streets I saw every day but had not talked to, and I pushed it for every man lying on an old mattress on an old bed in a five-by-seven plywood box with chicken wire on top.

I pushed the button until my arm tired, and I let my hand drop.

That little red button betrayed me. My articles on the homeless had made me a local hero of their cause, and when they were published by the Associated Press, I became a recognized advocate for the destitute and dispossessed, and an even bigger hero. When my article about Parker's operations in Mexico came out, I included a rousing endorsement of his attitude toward changing the upstream fundamentals that created homelessness, poverty, and illiteracy in the first place. That won me even more endorsement as an advocate for public solutions to social ills and as a strong representative of the people victimized by those problems.

But when Parker offered me his magic button, my deepest hidden feelings would have pushed it and dashed all those people into oblivion.

What would my readers think of me then?

I had never anticipated the weight that caring about the homeless brought, the ever-present awareness haunting me as I watched them on the streets every day, thinking about them continually, wanting a cure, a solution to their problems, and yet confessing I had not found even the crumbs of an answer that would make a difference.

As the heaviness—the burden—of having no solution settled on my shoulders, frustration swirled around me because I felt impotent. I was their representative: More was expected of me, because I was more responsible, more knowledgeable, more vocal, more in the van-guard of their cause. If the people I interviewed cried out in the wilderness, I needed to cry out with them. And yet, crying was all I could do.

Having been one of them during my time in the tube made me even more weary of my responsibility, and made me feel more useless.

Deep down inside, I wanted out.

I didn't want to be a hero anymore. Not all of me would have wanted to press Parker's button, but any little piece of me that hoped the magic would work was enough to display my hypocrisy.

No wonder my writing was going nowhere: The story was refusing to be told because being truthful would have revealed me for what I am. Parker had forced my finger down on the button he made—there was no question—but when I described that moment, where would I put the asterisk—the one leading you to the bottom of the page where it would state that, to be honest, a little bit of me didn't think Parker's magic button was such a bad idea. That it made sense in some situations. That, even as an advocate, I sometimes looked at the people on the street corners or the medians or sleeping in doorways or hustling tourists and thought that maybe, just maybe, it would be okay to have such a button, to press it and make them all disappear. It would be a new opportunity, a new chance to reset ourselves as a society, maybe to start over and know earlier what was coming so we could figure something out in time to prevent the homeless and the poor and the powerless and the disenfranchised in the first place.

Or maybe I wanted the red button to exist just to make them all go away so we could stop seeing them for a while. So *I* could stop seeing them for a while.

Without the asterisk, without those kinds of words to explain my feelings, whatever I wrote would be dishonest, hanging empty in the air and refusing to hide my guilt. It would have been only one side of the truth when the other side needed to be told as well—that sometimes compassion should be measured by the rate of return.

No return, no compassion.

I suddenly couldn't breathe. Jimmy's cardboard box was small and the air stifling. I scrambled out of the box, out of the building, out through the fence, out sucking in the air, out where I belonged.

I hunched over, my hands on my knees, struggling for breath, struggling to get back to equilibrium. I trudged down the alley to my car and pushed the button on the door handle. The car didn't open. I pressed again, and again. What the hell? I had a keyless lock. Maybe the battery had run down or something.

That's when I realized my key fob wasn't in my pocket.

Damn.

It must have fallen out of my pocket. In Jimmy's box, in Jimmy's house. Back there.

I took a deep breath, tried to be calm, walked back through the alley, through the fence, through the door, to the box, grabbed my fob off the floor, backed out of the box, and was gone.

I went home. In a hurry.
Now what?

CHAPTER 31

I WAS STILL FEELING CONFUSED, exposed, and humiliated sitting at Starbucks the next morning, mindlessly watching the traffic flow past the window. I felt like I was naked but no one else had noticed yet.

"Hey, you're the newspaper guy, right?"

A teenage girl had come up to my table. Nice, pretty, good smile.

"Yep, that's me," I said with a nod, happy I wasn't really naked.

She plopped down in the opposite chair.

"You wrote about my family. My mom's Sarah F."

Sarah F. She was the one whose carpenter husband had lost his job when the construction business went south. She and her family—the husband, a fourteen-year-old boy, a sixteen-year-old girl—had had to move to subsidized housing after defaulting on their mortgage.

"Yes, sure, I remember."

"Well, I'm Cindy, her daughter," she said as she scooted her backpack with her feet and leaned forward on the table. "I really liked your articles."

"Thank you. How are you and your family doing?"

"Oh, wow, you wouldn't believe it. Some big housing company bought MiraMax and started building again. They hired my dad back as a supervisor because he knew all the contractors. And even better, someone with the company who read your articles realized that some employees had lost their homes, so they put the old model homes up for sale way cheap because they weren't going to build those styles anymore anyway. And we got one!"

"My articles did that? Who would have thought? That's great news. I'm really happy for you. How's your mom doing?"

"Oh my god! You won't believe what she did. She talked the building people into hiring her to clean the houses after they finished their drywall work, then started her own company so she could bid on contracts for other cleaning jobs, too. Now she's as busy as my dad, and him being a contractor gives us all sorts of income tax deductions."

I was floored. "I'm very impressed. I bet your mom is a whiz at the work. I assume you're happier now?"

She gave a shy grin and nodded. "I started working for her, cleaning texture splatter off the windows and trim. I only work on Sunday afternoons and maybe an afternoon during the week, but guess what? I'm making my own money!"

I gave her a big grin. "It is nice being independently wealthy, right?"

She laughed. "I guess she told you I wanted all the teenager stuff, right? Well, your articles made me think about things. When I saw what my parents had gone through, I realized I'd been focusing on wanting things instead of figuring out what kind of person I wanted to be. I'd been avoiding the hard decisions. Now, if I want something bad enough, I'm going to work for it instead of expecting my mom and dad to give it to me. Pretty cool, huh?"

I agreed and drank her a toast.

"So, you ever hear from the others, the other people you interviewed?" she asked.

"Oh, not really. Well, you know the first one I talked to, Jimmy A? He died last week. Hit by a car while standing at his favorite panhandling spot. And you know I mentioned that Crazy Sally disappeared. I still don't know what happened to her.

"I haven't heard from anyone else. Looks like your family's the leading success story."

"Well, you made a big difference for us."

"I did what I could."

"I'd say what you did was a lot," Cindy said with a smile. "All it takes is good people to do good things. That's what my English teacher keeps saying."

"Well, that makes it true then. Never doubt an English teacher."

"Okay. Gotta run. Nice to see you," she said as she retrieved her backpack and hurried out the door.

Well. How about that. I got another coffee and donut and leaned back in my chair to think. What had Cindy said? Something about focusing on the kind of person she wanted to be instead of on wanting things. That was a hard decision for her to make.

I remembered Parker's lecture about hard decisions, calling himself the one who was willing to make them and the rest of us just cowards. Killing the homeless was a hard decision, he had said, but by making it, he'd solved the social and financial problems associated with them.

But that wasn't true, was it? The hard decision is deciding what kind of person you want to be. Somewhere along the line, Parker had decided it was okay to consider the homeless as worthless, and because they were worthless, they could be wiped off the face of the earth without guilt. I'm sure he would have extended the same thinking to other groups that didn't measure up to his standards: the intellectually challenged, the mentally ill, the illiterate, the foolish, the unborn.

After having made his assumption and declaring it to be true, all Parker had to do was solve the engineering problems. I'm sure he'd done a cost-benefit analysis and felt proud of how he managed the tradeoffs to get his answer: You kill them all.

But that was just engineering. Those were the easy decisions. The hard ones are deciding what kind of person you want to be.

It's the same flaw the red button had. In some ways, it seems so simple—no pain, no condemnation, no guilt, no responsibility, no blame, no remorse. If you ignore what his magic was based on—Parker's initial decision that the homeless have no value and thus, making them disappear has no cost—then you can press the button all day long and not feel bad.

That applies to everything in life: If there's no cost, you can do whatever you want.

But hard decisions always have costs; that's why they're hard. If a decision has consequences—if you have to make sacrifices, or tradeoffs, or it helps some people but hurts others, or if the answer solves only part of the problem, or forces you to acknowledge some truth—then what you end up with are costs: mental, physical, and emotional.

Parker wouldn't have admitted it, but his assumptions and decisions cost him dearly: He had to sacrifice his humanity. He had to be willing to abandon compassion, mercy, identity, love, values, beliefs, and a slew more of the intangibles that make us human—all to achieve nothing more than a solution that was easy to implement.

When I was inside Jimmy's box, pressing the red button over and over, I did it because I had been sucked in by Parker's mantra that it cost me nothing. I had been fooled in the same way he was fooled. What I knew now was the hard decision he thought he was making led him to the wrong answer. The real cost he paid was his humanity.

Disregarding a person's worth has a long list of personal and communal costs centered on who you are, who you believe you ought to be, and who you think other people should be. It costs to have principles and values and beliefs so you know how you want to treat others and how they should treat you.

Real life unavoidably, inescapably comes packaged with great cost—if it's free, it's not real.

The truth is, I want life to be full of hard decisions. I want to struggle with how my decisions impact the way others live and love and interact as they try their darnedest to make something of themselves or their family or their kids. I want my decisions to make enough of a difference that it takes wisdom to do it right.

I want people to have value, not effectiveness. I want worth, not productivity. I want presence, not contribution—intangibles, hard-won substance, and internal gold. I want hearts instead of hands, feelings instead of brains, tears instead of sweat, compassion instead of judgment, mercy instead of law. I want honor and devotion instead of social agreements. I want love with power. I want a chance for everyone to make something of themselves, to do great things.

If nothing else, I don't want to stand in their way.

I want life to be difficult so when I get it right—when I do make a diamond from a chunk of coal, hit one out of the ball-park, go for the glory—I'll find it a source of unimaginable joy. I want to experience exultation, wonder, breathtaking beauty. I want to be surprised by all the things in the world that come out wonderfully.

I shouldn't have been so hard on myself because my articles offered no good solution for homelessness. It's a hard problem to solve. What's important is there's a host of lesser solutions that can still make a difference. It can be something as simple as helping out at a soup kitchen, contributing money to a shelter, making survival bags—socks, soap, tooth-brushes, food cards, books, first aid packets, etc.—to hand out to the homeless on street corners. Or, for me, continuing to write articles that help people to find compassion and awareness within themselves.

If I had the talents and money of a Parker Evans, I could address problems at the planetary level. If I were president, I could do things for the nation. For the most part, though, I'm limited to the level I'm at, but whatever work I can do here is a hell of a lot better than patting some homeless guy on the back and encouraging him to have hope because there'll definitely be a social program coming along to help him out.

Next chance I get, I'll slip a buck into somebody's cup, or maybe even a twenty. They'll feel better, I can afford it, and we'll both have a better day as a result. And if somebody thinks I shouldn't be putting that money into that cup—because I'm not being considerate enough of tourists—I'll tell the judge that compassion and generosity are higher values and should be encouraged for everyone at every level. Making them illegal is beneath the dignity and humanity of us all.

———

My thoughts after Cindy left wrapped up a lot of the loose ends from my complicated dealings with Parker. My life fell back into place, and I became a whole and consistent person again, which Beth and the rest of my family were overwhelmingly glad to see. Realizing and confronting my fears of the red button and what it meant, facing the feelings it brought to the surface, made my writing problems melt away. I was once again banging away on my keyboard like a madman. My book advance came and allowed me to retire from the newspaper, which, with the money, gave me a sense of time and wealth I had never imagined.

As I was finishing Parker's book, I decided my next book would be different, a middle-grade story about a young girl who lives in poverty, has a bad family situation and eventually finds herself abandoned and alone on the streets. It will be fiction but loaded with reality.

The editors at Random House seem to think I'm a pretty good writer, so I expect they'll publish it. Then, with their marketing muscle, I'll sell it to young people and their families, as well as schools and libraries. There's a lot of people it can reach. I'll also give free copies to shelters, to social program directors, and to every church that helps the homeless.

I want children, parents, advisers, teachers, social workers, and governments to see what really happens when a child ends up in a position that, to most of us, is unimaginable. People need to know the reality of the situation, and the difference it can make if their hearts lead them to do something about it.

I would need an expert consultant to get reality into the story, so, as difficult as it was to track her down, I found the ideal person to provide a first-hand account. Remember Jamie E, the homeless eleven-year-old? She was hesitant to work with me since I would be writing words she could not read, but my wife and I offered to help get her through it. Over a number of consulting sessions, we eased her into staying at our house, with periodic visits to those who had been her caretakers.

It may seem strange that a couple as old as us would end up working with a girl the age of our grandchildren, but it was something we could do, and age was a secondary consideration. Jamie will be an adult soon enough, and a couple of people with experience might help her to make up for lost time. We figure she's just on loan to us anyway.

She liked having her own bed, a clean bathroom, fresh food, and other kids in the neighborhood. In fact, Jamie admitted at one point that having parents wasn't so bad after all, but she remained on the fence about any formal steps. That's when I remembered what she'd said about wishing for straight teeth. I hate to be accused of outright manipulation, but I took her to an orthodontist friend for an examination. No problem, he said, but it would take a couple of years to get everything adjusted. It called for more of a commitment from us to remain together for the duration, if only to make sure she kept all her appointments. But afterwards, I pointed out, she'd have a smile that even Beyoncé would admire.

That sealed the deal, and we became her official foster parents.

As I said, it was something we could do. When the papers were all done, my wife suggested the three of us celebrate with some sort of vacation, like a cruise.

Uh, that involves the ocean, right? How about Disney World, instead?

A LOOK AT SMOKE DREAMS

BY DONALD WILLERTON

A House with a Dark Past. A Man with a Broken Soul. Will Either Survive the Rebuild?

Tucker Whitby is no stranger to pain. Haunted by guilt over his wife's death and his daughter's brutal murder, he's thrown himself into his work as a builder. But when he's tasked with remodeling a house that seems to be alive—breathing, pulsing, and violently reactive—he faces more than just a construction challenge. The house has its own plans.

As Tucker uncovers the property's eerie history, he's pulled into vivid dreams of a boy kidnapped by Comanche warriors in 1870. But the dreams soon blur with reality, and Tucker finds himself living the boy's violent, harrowing life. As the line between past and present dissolves, Tucker is drawn into a spiral of violence and murder, uncovering secrets that threaten to consume him.

Can Tucker break free from the house's grip, or will it rebuild him in ways he never imagined?

Discover the chilling thriller that will keep you on the edge of your seat. Grab your copy now and unravel the mystery before it's too late.

AVAILABLE NOW

ABOUT THE AUTHOR

New Mexico-based Donald Willerton is the author of *Death in the Tallgrass*, the winner of the Western Writers of America 2024 SPUR Award for Western Historical Fiction, a finalist in the 2024 American Fiction Awards, and a finalist in the 2024 Storytrade Book Awards. He has written a ten-book Middle Grade/Young Adult mystery series located in the Southwest, two contemporary thrillers, and a fictional World War II adventure novel. To finance his writing, he used his degrees in physics and computer science as a scientist, manager, and computer specialist, but has always let his curiosity, imagination, and passion for history keep his head aligned with his heart.